I0600530

Who's Under Where?

by Marcia Kash
&
Doug Hughes

A SAMUEL FRENCH ACTING EDITION

SAMUEL FRENCH

FOUNDED 1830

New York Hollywood London Toronto

SAMUELFRENCH.COM

ISBN 978-0-573-69389-2   Printed in U.S.A.   #25680

ACKNOWLEDGMENTS

Who's Under Where? is an original work by the authors based on material originally conceived by Ian Clark, Ian Deakin, Cheryl Hood, Marcia Kash and Cheryl Partington.

iii

IMPORTANT BILLING AND CREDIT REQUIREMENTS

All producers of WHO'S UNDER WHERE? *must* give credit to the Author of the Play in all programs distributed in connection with performances of the Play and in all instances in which the title of the Play appears for purposes of advertising, publicizing or otherwise exploiting the Play and/or a production The name of the Author *must* also appear on a separate line, on which no other name appears, immediately following the title, and *must* appear in size of type not less than fifty percent the size of the title type

Who's Under Where? was first performed at The Muskoka Festival, Gravenhurst, Ontario, Canada, on July 27th 1992, with the following cast of characters:

Jane Pritchard ....Jane Moffat
Sybil Brunt ....Mary Long
Paul Pritchard ....Michael Lamport
George Brunt ....Ian D. Clark
Sebastian..Michael Cram
Roger Hodge......................................Colin Miller
Bruno Fruferelli ....Richard Farrell

Directed by..................................Ronald R. Ulrich
Set Design ....Joelle Davis
Lighting Design ....Brad Trenaman
Costume Design ....Kathryn Immonen
Stage Manager ....Theresa Malek

CHARACTERS
(in order of appearance)

Jane Pritchard —   Early-to-mid-thirties. Attractive, lively. Designer and co-owner of Passion Fashion Wear.

Sybil Brunt: Mid-to-late-thirties, attractive, organized. Marketing director, co-owner and the driving force behind Passion Fashion Wear.

Paul Pritchard: Early forties, divorce lawyer. Smart, attractive. Married to Jane.

George Brunt: Mid-forties, college professor. Trusting, amiable, a little out of shape. Married to Sybil.

Sebastian: Early twenties. Tall, gorgeous, built. Very butch. Typical male model.

Roger Hodge: British, fifties. Career security officer. Upright, by-the-book type.

Bruno Fruferelli: Italian, early fifties. Roly-poly, attractive. VERY charming. Accomplished businessman. Very wealthy.

TIME & PLACE

The action of the play takes place in a luxurious hotel suite. The time is the present.

The scene opens onto a luxurious, fifth-floor hotel suite. UC are a couple of steps leading to a pair of French windows which open onto a balcony upon which are at least two large potted plants. Visibility through the windows must be as close to perfect as possible. SR is the main entrance. A large, sturdy Chinese screen is US of the door, with easy accessibility from both sides. There is also a small table with a full-length tablecloth and a telephone on one side of the screen. DSL is the bathroom exit. USL is a door leading to the bedroom. Other appropriate furniture as space permits. DSR is a love seat and armchair with a small coffee table. There are a number of boxes scattered around the room, and piles of lingerie on various surfaces. There is also a rolling rack with a selection of outfits hanging on it.

JANE is discovered leaning on the vanity, talking on the phone with Lorraine, the seamstress. SHE lifts a pile of lingerie from the vanity and discovers an assortment of 8x10's of male models underneath. SHE becomes engrossed with the photos, sorting through them one by one, oblivious to her task.

JANE. (*Excited.*) Lorraine, you're a lifesaver. We can't thank you enough .... Yes, it's all here. ... I told you, the courier's just arrived with the samples .... You must have been sewing in your sleep to get all this finished. I just hope Sybil and I can get everything else ready before Fruferelli arrives. I still can't believe he's coming here specially to see us. I'm so excited I can't think straight—

(*Holding up one of the photos.*) OH MY GOD! ... No, it's nothing, I've just seen another of these gorgeous models Sybil left me in charge of picking one of them for this afternoon and I'm having the hardest time. Actually, I'm having the time of my life! This one's called "Forrest." He's leaning on a surfboard or something. He's wearing this sexy string bikini thing and he has a body ... no, Lorraine, he's not here in person, it's just a picture . you know, an 8x10 shot ... inches ... Lorraine, you have a filthy mind .... They're models the agency submitted for the showing with Fruferelli this afternoon. I've hired three so far ... yes, I know, she'll kill me when she finds out, but what's a girl to do? You should see these guys! They're like potato chips. How can you have just one?

(*SYBIL enters carrying a large box of lingerie samples.*)

JANE. Oh, Sybil's back, Lorraine, and she's got the goodies. I'd better go. Thanks again! You're an angel. I'll call you back when we're all millionaires Millionaire-esses. Bye! (*Hangs up the phone.*)

SYBIL. (*Setting the box on the coffee table and opening it.*) That woman is a saint. I don't know how she does it. Yesterday, these were a few drawings on a sketch pad And today, VOILA! (*SHE pulls something slinky out of the box.*)

JANE. (*Races over with Forrest's 8x10*) Oooooh, let me see those. (*SHE looks at the photo then at the briefs then back at the photo.*) MMmmm.

SYBIL. What in Heaven's name are you doing?

JANE. Just a little creative visualization. It's healthy. You should try it sometime.

SYBIL. Oh I do, darling. I just visualize different things.

JANE. Like the five million bucks we stand to make if we pull this deal off.

(SYBIL knocks on the coffee table.)

JANE. *(Looking toward door.)* Who is it?

SYBIL. It's me.

JANE. Will you stop doing that? You sound like a woodpecker in heat!

SYBIL I can't help it. You make me nervous when you say things like that. I'm terrified you're going to jinx us. I know it seems silly, but I don't want to tempt Fate. I'm having a hard enough time believing all this as it is.

JANE. I know what you mean. It doesn't seem possible, does it? A couple of months ago Passion Fashion Wear was a modestly successful lingerie business and then—

SYBIL. And then we met Signor Fruferelli and now we're on our way to making a fortune.

SYBIL. Come on, let's get to work.

(JANE starts sorting new stuff on racks. Throughout the rest of the scene THEY are both busy arranging the outfits, tidying the room, etc.)

SYBIL. *(Examining female lingerie on rack.)* How far have you got with these?

JANE. Well, I've got the Wet Dreams on the rack, together with the Honeymoon Hots and the Quickies.

SYBIL. I've told you before, they are not the "Wet Dreams," they are the "Teenage Fantasies." And we don't

call them the "Quickies" either; they are the Forbidden
Passion line.

JANE. (*Shaking out a sporty pair of men's boxers.*) I
know, I know, and our new Just for the Gym line isn't
called "Jumping Jocks."

SYBIL. Oh, by the way, which one of those models
have you chosen?

JANE. (*Evasively.*) Models? Oh, models! Yes.
Speaking of models, I almost forgot. Suzanne phoned.
She's running a little late. She said she'd probably be here
by three.

SYBIL. Damn. Well never mind about Suzanne,
Fruferelli saw most of the female stuff at the trade show.
I'm more concerned about the male model. (*Going through
photos.*) Which one did you pick?

JANE. Gee, I'd forgotten how much of this stuff there
was! This is going to take me forever to sort out.

SYBIL. I hope he's not too short, whoever he is.
Suzanne's a giant. We don't want her towering over him.

JANE. (*Still sorting.*) Oh don't worry, they're all over
six feet.

SYBIL. All?

JANE. Yes. Well all the ones I picked are.

SYBIL. ALL?

(*JANE giggles, gives a shrug.*)

SYBIL. Jane. Darling. Fruferelli is going to be here
within the hour and we haven't even finished unpacking
yet! We've barely managed to finish the samples. We've
lied to our husbands, blown our savings, and put our
business on the line for this one shot at the big time We

don't have time for guessing games. So tell me, which one have you picked?

JANE. Sybil, relax! I've narrowed it down to three.

SYBIL. THREE? What do we need three of them for?

JANE. Well what self-respecting lingerie designer does a show with only one model?

SYBIL. I noticed you haven't booked any more female models.

JANE. He saw our female line at the trade show! And he was sufficiently impressed with it to want to see the male line. He's flying into town today especially to see these (*Holds up male samples.*) on bodies. And you can't do that with just one model can you? It's like hiring a fiddler to play a string quartet!

SYBIL. You're right. I shouldn't have doubted your judgement.

JANE. Besides, Fruferelli said "I wanta to see these ina da flesh." Well we're going to give him all the flesh he can handle.

SYBIL. All the flesh you can handle, you mean.

JANE. Come on, Sybil, if we're going to invest our life's savings in this little venture, we might as well have a few perks along the way.

SYBIL. (*Indicating photos.*) Perks? Don't you mean "pecs"?

JANE. Well, why not?

SYBIL. What about Paul?

JANE. What Paul doesn't know won't hurt me!

SYBIL. When I suggested that we keep this from the guys I did it for noble and humble reasons.

JANE. You did not. You did it to save face in case it doesn't work out.

SYBIL. It's not as simple as that. You remember the campaign that ended my advertising career—the Barton Gimble account?

JANE. The smelly feet people?

SYBIL. The foot powder people. Nodorex.

JANE. Oh yeah. The ad with the kick line of sweaty socks. I thought it was a great idea.

SYBIL. So did the folks at Barton Gimble. In fact, they were so enthusiastic, I was sure it was a done deal.

JANE. I know, I know, and you went home and told George, and he snuck out and bought you that brand-new BMW to celebrate—

SYBIL. And the next day, I walk into the office, and find that the Nodorex account has become the ex-Nodorex account.

JANE. Well, look at the bright side. You got a BMW out of the deal.

SYBIL. George was such a sweetheart about the whole thing. He put up with so much—my resignation, my depression, my guilt—

JANE. Your car payments ...

SYBIL. Precisely.

JANE. It's a good thing he has tenure.

SYBIL. You're not kidding ... and if he knew what was at stake here today, he'd probably go out and buy me a football stadium. And that's why I haven't told him.

JANE. That and the fact that you're superstitious as hell.

SYBIL. I don't recall you making any objections when I asked you to keep this a secret.

JANE. I have my own reasons for keeping my mouth shut—even if they aren't as noble and humble as yours.

SYBIL Uh-huh.

JANE There is only one thing in the world that will give me more satisfaction than closing this deal—and that is seeing the look on Paul's face when I show him the contract. He'll probably think I'm putting him on—the idea that someone could make that kind of money selling underwear—

SYBIL. Lingerie—

JANE. —is beyond his comprehension.

SYBIL He's never taken our work very seriously, has he?

JANE. He just doesn't get it. His philosophy seems to be that if you're wearing something to bed, you need it to keep warm.

SYBIL. How ironic. He's married to one of the most talented lingerie designers on the planet, and he likes to sleep in the nude.

JANE. Philistine.

SYBIL. By the way, how did he react when you told him we'd be visiting my mother again today?

JANE. He didn't bat an eyelash.

SYBIL. You're kidding.

JANE. No—I couldn't believe he fell for that line again. In fact, he didn't just fall for it, he was actually encouraging me to go.

SYBIL That's funny. I had the same experience with George. And you know how George feels about my mother.

JANE I guess they were too preoccupied with their fishing trip. Paul was all hot to trot about it this morning You should have seen him at breakfast—he was done up in that silly fishing outfit of his—he couldn't wait to get started. He was out the door before I was.

SYBIL. (*Picking up the photos.*) How did you decide which of these guys to settle on? They all look the same. Well almost. My God, this one isn't wearing anything at all. Oh wait, now I see it. Just.

JANE. Well, it was tough, but I've narrowed it down to these ... (*Holds up three photos and crossing to Sybil to show her.*) Number one—Peter.

SYBIL. How appropriate.

JANE. Look, it even has Peter's measurements listed here.

SYBIL. Those aren't his measurements, it's his height in inches and centimeters.

JANE. Sounds impressive whatever they are! Anyway, here's number two—Cliff.

SYBIL. What's he doing with that goat?

JANE. I don't know, it's one of those outdoorsy-type photos. They all pose with wildlife.

SYBIL. Are you sure we phoned the right number?

JANE. (*Admiring photo.*) I thought he'd look great in our "Lumber Slumber" line.

SYBIL. Who, Cliff or the goat?

JANE. Don't be perverse. And here's ba-aa-aa-chelor number three—Sebastian.

SYBIL. Ooh, look, he's dropped his ball.

JANE. No he hasn't, he's dribbling.

SYBIL. Now who's being perverse?

JANE. No, not dribbling (*Indicates mouth.*)—Dribbling (*Miming dribbling a basketball.*).

SYBIL. Dribbling. Hmm. Well, they all look fine to me. What time are they arriving?

JANE. They'll call from downstairs when they arrive. I told them to be here for three.

SYBIL. Fine. Now, champagne.

JANE. Isn't it a little early to be celebrating?

SYBIL. It's not for us you nitwit, it's for Fru-Fru.

JANE So that's the plan, is it? Get him up to our fancy hotel room and get him drunk? Well, I suppose it's one way of making the deal.

SYBIL. I have no intention of getting him drunk—just happy. The more we give him what he likes, the more he likes what we give him, know what I mean?

JANE. Fine. But why champagne?

SYBIL. It's the only thing he drinks

JANE. I think I could get used to that.

(SYBIL goes to phone and dials. JANE proceeds to tidy up the empty boxes.)

SYBIL. Hello, room service? ... This is Sybil Brunt in room 504. Could you send up a couple of bottles—make that three bottles of your best champagne ... Thank you.

JANE Three? He won't be happy, he'll be dead.

SYBIL. We don't want to be caught short.

JANE. Err on the side of caution, I always say. I've finished with these boxes.

SYBIL. Great. Let's put them in the bedroom. (*As SHE bends to picks up a box SHE lets out a squeal.*) Oh no!

JANE. What ?

SYBIL. Look at the size of this run. (*SHE indicates a large run in her nylons.*)

JANE. That's not a run, it's a marathon.

SYBIL. I don't have time for this.

JANE. Not to worry—I just happen to have a spare pair in the bedroom. Follow me. (*SHE picks up a couple of boxes and heads for the bedroom.*)

SYBIL. You are a darling. (*SYBIL follows her in and closes the door.*)

(*We hear SCRABBLING and SCRATCHING from behind the main door, accompanied by a lot of GRUNTING and GROANING. Suddenly, an American Express card comes shooting through the crack in the door.*)

PAUL . (*Offstage.*) Shit!

(*There is a muffled conversation on the other side of the door. More SCRABBLING and SCRATCHING. Finally, the door opens. Paul and GEORGE peer in briefly and disappear. THEY appear again, checking the room, and disappear once more. PAUL rushes in and hides behind the sofa. HE beckons to George, who follows. BOTH are dressed in fishing gear of some kind. GEORGE is carrying a portable video camera in one hand and something resembling a credit card in the other. Their heads pop up above the sofa. THEY look in either direction and pop down again. Their heads appear again, looking in different directions, then to each other. THEY scream and disappear. They then pop up again. PAUL crosses to the Amex card and picks it up.*)

PAUL. I guess they don't take American Express here. What did you use, anyway?

GEORGE. (*Holding card up.*) My trusty Blood Donor card—don't leave home without it.

PAUL. You'd better wipe that card, George.

GEORGE What for?

PAUL. For prints.

GEORGE But it's my own card—it's got my blood type on it, for God's sake!

PAUL. Yes, you're right. We'd better destroy it.

GEORGE. What?

PAUL. It's evidence. We've just committed a crime here, my friend.

GEORGE. Well, I won't tell anybody if you won't.

PAUL. (*Getting up.*) It's not you I'm worried about. It's the hotel security. If they catch us in here, we're dead.

GEORGE. Well then—maybe we'd better close the door

PAUL. Why did you leave it open?

GEORGE. You didn't tell me to close it.

PAUL. Do I have to tell you everything?

GEORGE. (*As HE crosses and closes the door.*) You're the expert. If I were in charge, we'd be on the lake by now.

PAUL. (*Wandering around the room.*) I wonder what this room is costing them. (*HE steps out onto the balcony.*) What a view! George, come and look at this.

(*GEORGE follows him out and shuts the door. THEY both admire the view. The bedroom door opens and the WOMEN enter talking.*)

SYBIL. What a relief. Now where were we?

JANE. Running out of time, as I recall.

SYBIL. (*Checking her watch.*) Right. We'd better go down and get the other boxes from the car. When we get back we can figure out what to put our male models into.

JANE. I'm not going to touch that one.
SYBIL. I'd rather you didn't touch any-one!
JANE. Spoilsport!

(THEY exit through main door.
PAUL and GEORGE re-enter. GEORGE is fiddling with
the camera. PAUL goes to examine the lingerie.)

GEORGE. This zoom is great. I think I can see my
house from here.
PAUL. Will you stop wasting valuable film? (*HE picks
up a handful of lingerie.*) Good God, look at all this stuff!
GEORGE. (*Indicating camera.*) Paul, do you think this
is really necessary?
PAUL. (*Examining lingerie.*) Doesn't do anything for
me.
GEORGE. No, no, no, I mean the camera.
PAUL. Oh. Absolutely. (*Takes the camera from him.*)
We need some evidence. Catching them red-handed isn't
enough. It's still their word against ours.
GEORGE. I'm not so sure I want to catch them red-
handed. I don't think I want to catch them red-anythinged
I'd rather just confront them
PAUL. (*Shooting the room, the lingerie, etc.*) If we
confront them, they'll only one, pretend nothing is wrong,
two, deny everything, and three, attack us. We have to
have proof. Red hot proof.
GEORGE. (*Holding a pair of flaming red bikini briefs
up to the camera.*) I think we've got that.
PAUL. (*Putting the camera down.*) I'll take those,
thank you very much. (*PAUL takes the briefs from George,*

gets a glassene bag out of his tackle box, puts the briefs in it, and returns the bag to the tackle box.)

GEORGE. You're the lawyer, so correct me if I'm wrong, but aren't people supposed to be presumed innocent until proven guilty?

PAUL. They've proven themselves guilty.

GEORGE. How?

PAUL. They've lied to us. Take today for example—they told us they were spending the day with Sybil's mother.

GEORGE. Yes, and we told them we were going fishing.

PAUL. That's different!

GEORGE. Why?

PAUL. Well, because ... because they started it!

GEORGE. Oh, very good. Do you win many cases with logic like that?

PAUL. The point is, they're deceiving us. They've been deceiving us for God knows how long! And if catching them out means telling the odd fib, well, that's perfectly justified as far as I'm concerned *(PAUL looks around some more and discovers the bedroom.)*

GEORGE. I'm still not convinced that they have been deceiving us. I mean, they are in this line of work, after all They're bound to carry lots of samples around with them This is probably just some kind of business meeting.

PAUL. *(Pointing through the open door.)* You're so gullible, George If it's a business meeting, why do they need a King size waterbed?

(GEORGE goes into the bedroom.)

PAUL. And why didn't they tell us what they were doing? Why all the secrecy? They obviously have something to hide—George, will you get up? This is no time for a siesta!

GEORGE. (*Coming out and closing the door.*) I'd get seasick sleeping on that thing.

PAUL Will you stop fooling around! They've been behaving very suspiciously for weeks.

GEORGE. So they've come home from work late once in a while—

PAUL. George, I've seen it a hundred times. The signs are always the same For example—when was the last time Sybil was home for dinner?

GEORGE. Well, we went out for Chinese last Thursday—

PAUL. Doesn't count. When was the last time you had dinner together at home?

GEORGE. ... I can't remember.

PAUL. Right Now, have you had any strange phone calls lately? Say, people hanging up on you, or strange men calling and asking to speak to Sybil?

GEORGE. The odd one, I suppose ...

PAUL. And when you question her about these calls, does she get uncomfortable, or evasive or vague?

GEORGE. (*Uncertain.*) A little, I guess.

PAUL. And when was the last time you and Sybil had sex?

GEORGE What does that have to do with anything?

PAUL. When was the last time you and Sybil had sex?

GEORGE. Uh—

PAUL. Bingo. Haven't you noticed how every weekend for the past couple of months, they've had some excuse to vanish—some alibi to account for their time away from home?

GEORGE. Yes, but—

PAUL. That's why I suggested we play along with them today. And as you can see, instead of finding them visiting with Sybil's mother, we find them in a ritzy hotel room full of sexy underwear. Doesn't that seem a trifle suspicious to you?

GEORGE. Perhaps ...

PAUL. I'm telling you George, I've seen this too many times to just dismiss it.

GEORGE. You've prosecuted too many divorce cases. In your own jargon, this is all circumstantial.

PAUL. Correct. That's why we're here. We need something we can take to court.

GEORGE. We're not talking about a couple of bank robbers here, we're talking about our wives! (*Hovers above the coffee table.*) I mean, who are we to spy on them like this? Who are we to pass judgement on them? Who are we to accuse them of deceit? (*Sees one of the photos and picks it up.*) Who the hell is this?

PAUL. (*Crossing to look at the picture.*) Good God! (*HE flips through the rest of the pictures.*) Looks like they've got a busy day planned. I wonder if they're going to have them all at once or one at a time.

GEORGE. What are you talking about?

PAUL. (*Grabbing the photos.*) No wonder they're out late all the time. No wonder they're distracted. No wonder they're not interested in us anymore. They've discovered the excitement of illicit sex. I know all about it.

GEORGE. (*Curiously.*) Really?

PAUL. I make my living dealing with this. The agencies, the photographs, the coded phone conversations. I just can't believe Jane is capable of going this far.

GEORGE. (*Indicating photos.*) Did you see the one with the goat?

PAUL. George, for God's sake! Don't you realize the seriousness of all this? Don't you know how bad this is?

GEORGE. How bad is it?

PAUL. How bad is it? How bad is it? George. Sybil and Jane have taken to buying sex from young, handsome, virile gigolos. Bad enough for you?

GEORGE. How can you be so sure? I mean, this could all be perfectly innocent.

PAUL. Yeah, sure, explain it to me. Add up all the clues and convince me it's innocent.

GEORGE. Well, I'm not sure about the rest of it but these photos here, they could just be a—I don't know, a collection, like some men have, of *Playboy* centerfolds.

PAUL. (*Indicating their surroundings.*) Who goes to this kind of trouble and expense just to look at a few pictures?

GEORGE. I don't know. It all seems so ludicrous. I just can't accept that Sybil would do this.

PAUL. What's the alternative?

GEORGE. (*Thinks for a second.*) Perhaps they aren't buying sex at all. Perhaps they're selling it!

PAUL Thank you very much. I feel better already.

GEORGE. There has to be some other explanation.

PAUL. I'm telling you the proof is mounting.

GEORGE. There's an unfortunate choice of words.

(The TELEPHONE rings. The MEN jump out of their skins. Finally PAUL picks it up.)

PAUL. *(Funny accent.)* Yes ... er, yes this is 504 ... No, she isn't here right now ... yes ... right ... thank you. *(HE hangs up.)* That was room service They are having some trouble locating the keys to the wine cellar so the champagne we ordered will be a bit delayed.

GEORGE. Right. *(Pause)* What champagne?

PAUL. Going all out, aren't they? Champagne eh? Still don't believe that they're up to no good?

GEORGE. I didn't say they weren't up to no good. I just hope to God they're not paying for it.

PAUL. What bloody difference does that make?

GEORGE. Look, they're only photographs. If they materialize into *men* I may subscribe to your theory. But for now, I'm giving Sybil the benefit of the doubt.

(The PHONE rings. THEY take to the phone. PAUL marches over and picks it up.)

PAUL. *(Chinese accent.)* Hello .. yes this is 504 ... No, she isn't here at the moment. Who are you? . . Who? ... *(Own voice.)* Early for what? ... *(Pleasantly, in his own voice.)* Oh really? Well, I'm afraid there's been a change of plan. Your appointment has been cancelled. Sorry .... Look buddy, you can just forget it ... I don't care what other "gigs" you've given up to come here, you show up at this room and you'll be doing your next gig in Intensive Care! Need me to spell that out for you? ... How much? ... HOW MUCH?... Fine . . you get your "agent" to sort out the money ... fine. *(HE hangs up.)*

GEORGE. Who was that?

PAUL. That was Peter. He was the three o'clock appointment, here a little early. (*HE looks at his watch.*) I'll say. Eager little fellow. Wants to be "paid for his time" even though he didn't "do anything."

GEORGE. Oh, my God.

PAUL. And when I threatened him, he said his "agent" would sort out the money with Mrs. Brunt. Can you believe the gall of that man? Three hundred bucks an hour he wants! I mean, he still expects to be paid, and he hasn't even done the job!

GEORGE Personally, I'd prefer it that way.

PAUL. And on top of that, he wants money for parking!

GEORGE. Parking what?

PAUL. (*Shoots George a look.*) Oh, shut up.

GEORGE. Anyway, I don't think you should have done that.

PAUL. Done what?

GEORGE. Scared him off. You're the one who keeps going on about proof, about catching them with their knickers down, if you'll pardon the expression

PAUL. Well, what did you expect me to do? Invite him up for tea?

GEORGE. Wasn't that the point? To catch him with his hands in the cookie jar?

PAUL. The last thing I want to see is someone else's hands all over my wife's cookies.

GEORGE. You should have let him come up—let them get on with it. Get it all on tape, get the hard evidence.

PAUL. (*Looking at one of the photos.*) I don't think I could face that.

GEORGE. (*Looking around the room at the bewildering array of lingerie.*) What do you think they were planning with this guy? A menage à trois?

PAUL. Looks to me like a menage à twelve.

(We hear the wives' voices outside the door.)

PAUL. They're back!

(The MEN run around the room in a panic.)

GEORGE. (*From the balcony door.*) Here! Here! Let's admire the view!

(GEORGE and PAUL run out onto the balcony.)

GEORGE. Camera!

(PAUL dives back into the room, grabs the camera, throws it to GEORGE, takes the tackle box and hurtles out the balcony door. HE closes it just as the WOMEN enter carrying boxes of lingerie. For the rest of the scene the TWO MEN are attempting to watch the events taking place in the room without being seen. N.B. They are unable to hear anything Neither can they be heard.)

SYBIL. Well, that's everything.

JANE. How are we going to work this?

SYBIL. Easy—we already know which of the male outfits we want modelled so you figure out which guy should wear what. I'll pull the companion pieces for Suzanne.

(JANE crosses to the table and picks up the photos of the three models.)

SYBIL. I've picked out some of the simpler lines for her—I want the focus to be on the men.

JANE. I can deal with that.

SYBIL. Come on, you'd better get these fellows dressed.

JANE. It's a dirty job, but someone's got to do it.

(JANE marches over to the couch. As she does so, the HUSBANDS' heads appear from behind cover out on the balcony.)

JANE. *(Holding the pictures in front of herself, one in each hand, and one under her chin.)* OK Syb—who's your favorite?

SYBIL. *(Carefully scrutinizing the photos.)* That one— *(SHE points.)* Sebastian, is it? The one who's drooling.

JANE. Dribbling.

SYBIL. Whatever.

JANE. Alright, Sebastian goes first, Cliff goes second, and Peter goes third. Great. Now what are we going to put you into, Sebastian my love?

(JANE plants a kiss on Sebastian's photo. The HUSBANDS react to this. JANE then turns to pick up the men's lingerie. As she turns, the HUSBANDS dive for cover.)

SYBIL. Let's put him in the Turquoise Temptation.

(JANE rummages through men's outfits on couch. The HUSBANDS stick their heads out from behind the potted plants and watch this.)

JANE. Which one's that? *(SHE holds up a pair of turquoise briefs.)* Oh, yes. One of my favorites. "Aqua Scrotum."

SYBIL. Could you hold those up for me? *(JANE drapes outfit in front of herself.)* Yes, that will do fine.

(SYBIL crosses to her notepad. The MEN reappear on the balcony.)

JANE. *(Caressing the briefs.)* Just feel this. It's like butter. *(Strokes her cheek with it.)* Mmmm. I must get a pair of these for Paul.

(PAUL and GEORGE react to this.)

SYBIL. *(Writing it down.)* Super. That's combination number one.

JANE. Fine. Where should I put them?

SYBIL. Um ...we can't use the bedroom, it's a disaster area in there. I think we'll give the men the bathroom to change in. They'll need more room, what with there being *three* of them. Suzanne can use the screen.

JANE. Sounds good to me.

(SHE sets Sebastian's outfit back on the couch. SYBIL turns to cross to the screen. The MEN scramble for cover.)

SYBIL. (*Hanging the negligee on the back of the screen*) Right. Number 2.

JANE. (*Holding up photo*) Cliff. The guy with the goat.

SYBIL. Let's put him in the Midnight Matador number.

JANE. No, not that number. The Lumber Slumber, remumber? (*SIC.*)

SYBIL. (*Rolls her eyes.*) Oh, alright. (*JANE pulls a matching flannel robe and boxers in a Lumberjack pattern and holds it in front of herself.*) In that case, let's put Suzanne in this (*Holds up a short, 2-piece peignoir.*)

JANE. What did we call that one? Oh, yes. "Hot To Trot"?

SYBIL. It's called "Anticipation." Lord, you have a one-track mind.

(*We see the potted PLANTS behind which George and Paul are hiding move toward the French doors.*)

SYBIL. We must remember to tell Suzanne and Rock—

JANE. Cliff.

SYBIL. Cliff—to take their robes off.

JANE. (*Crossing to couch to get Peter's photo and third outfit.*) Oh, don't worry, darling. I'll make sure Cliff gets that message.

SYBIL. Just make sure he knows enough to let Fru Fru see the shorts. Right—that's Combo Number 2.

(*The PHONE rings.*)

SYBIL. (*Picking up phone.*) Hello? ... Sebastian! ... You're here already? That's great. Come on up. We're in room 504 ... Fine. 'Bye *(Hangs up.)* What are we going to do with him? There's still so much to be done.

JANE. Don't worry—this is perfect We can get him to try on some of the things we're still working on before Fruferelli gets here.

SYBIL That's a terrific idea.

JANE. *(Pulling a pair of plaid boxers with a sporan on the front out of a box.)* Like the McUndies.

SYBIL. The Tartan Titans? Yes. And I want to see if the novelty items work. Did we bring the Christmas stuff?

(The MEN have a conversation behind the leaves. The PLANTS shake.)

JANE. The Mooning Santas? Are you kidding? Even I know better than that. *(Holding up a pair of briefs with a cotton tail on the back and bunny ears on the front.)* We did bring the Bugs Bunnies, though.

(PAUL and GEORGE exchange puzzled looks.)

SYBIL. *(Giggling.)* Peter Cottontail? Oh no, please, you can't be serious.

JANE Come on Syb, be a sport. I'm dying to see what they look like on

SYBIL. If you're so anxious to see them on, why don't you get Paul to model them for you?

JANE. Don't laugh—he's getting a pair for his birthday.

(There is a KNOCK on the door. SYBIL crosses to open it.)

SYBIL. Sebastian, I presume. I'm Sybil Brunt. Please come in.

(SEBASTIAN enters. HE's a young, handsome, well-built, typical square-jawed model.)

SEBASTIAN. Thank you.

JANE. *(Crossing to Sebastian.)* Hello, I'm Jane Pritchard. *(JANE offers her hand. It is still holding the Peter Cottontails. SHE tosses them onto a chair.)*

SEBASTIAN. Pleased to meet you. I hope you don't mind me being a little early.

SYBIL. Not at all. We're just selecting your outfits, as it happens. But listen, as long as you're here, we have a few items we've never seen modelled. Would you mind trying them on for us? They won't be in the show.

SEBASTIAN. Sure.

(JANE and SYBIL turn away and start rummaging through the stock. SEBASTIAN immediately starts to remove his clothes. Meanwhile, back on the balcony, PAUL and GEORGE are flabbergasted. THEY grab the camera and start filming. GEORGE is shooting while PAUL is playing director, pointing and motioning frantically JANE turns, sees Sebastian shirtless and removing his pants, and gasps audibly.)

SYBIL. *(Turning.)* AAAAGHH! Ah. Um, Sebastian, would you mind doing that in the bathroom?

SEBASTIAN. *(Shrugs.)* Sure What do you want me to change into?

JANE. Oh yes, of course. Forgot about that, didn't we? How about these, for a start? (*SHE hands him the Tartan Titans.*)

SEBASTIAN. Which door?

JANE. (*Pointing.*) That one.

SEBASTIAN. No problem.

(*HE picks up his clothes and exits into the bathroom. The WOMEN watch him go. Meanwhile, PAUL and GEORGE have encountered a problem with the camera, and do not see Sebastian exit. Throughout the following, THEY fiddle with the camera.*)

SYBIL. God, look at the time.

JANE. (*Looking toward bathroom door.*) What?

SYBIL. I said, "Look at the time." We've got to get a move on.

JANE. Right. Where were we?

SYBIL. Combination number 3.

(*Meanwhile, PAUL has opened the camera. HE is trying to deal with all the tape spewing out of it. In his frustration HE hurls the camera over the balcony. GEORGE tries to strangle Paul. THEY fall to the floor, and throughout the following we see their legs kicking as they fight.*)

JANE. Oh, yes. Not to worry—I've got Peter's PJs all picked out. (*Holds up a pair of very slinky-looking silk black-and-red pyjamas with little epaulets.*) Midnight Matador.

SYBIL. (*Pulls a frilly, red, vaguely Spanish-looking short nightie off the rack*) And in keeping with the bullfighting theme, Suzanne gets to wear this.

JANE. Oh, yes. The naughty Spanish thing.

SYBIL. (*Crossing and hanging the nightie on the back of the screen and scribbling in her notepad.*) The Scarlet Senorita. Wonderful.

(*The bathroom door opens, and SEBASTIAN enters wearing only the Tartan boxers.*)

SEBASTIAN. Here I am.

(*The WOMEN turn. HE does a brief walk up and down.*)

JANE. Oh, God!

SYBIL. Jane, settle down.

JANE. No, it's not that—look at them! They're way too long! I've got to put a hem on them. Give me some pins.

(*SYBIL hands her a pin-holder. The MEN reappear just in time to see JANE kneeling down in front of Sebastian. NB—Jane and Sebastian should be positioned so that he has his back to the French doors.*)

JANE. (*With her mouth full of pins.*) Now, hold still.

(*SHE takes a pin and starts to hem the boxers. SYBIL continues to straighten up the room.*)

JANE. Sybil, could you find me a needle and thread so I can tack these up, please?

SYBIL. Certainly (*Leaning on Sebastian's shoulder, seductively*) Boy, I'm glad you came early.

(*At this point, JANE accidentally jabs Sebastian with a pin. SEBASTIAN screams and tries to back away JANE grabs him, inadvertently holding him by the buns, to keep him in place. SEBASTIAN stands still, his arms thrust out sideways. PAUL and GEORGE look on in horror. PAUL is apoplectic. GEORGE is trying to reason with him.*)

JANE. I'm sorry. I guess I'm a little nervous. Hold still—I'm nearly done—there. (*SHE stands, backs up and admires her handiwork.*)

JANE. That's perfect What do you think, Sybil?

SYBIL. (*Handing Jane a needle and thread.*) Oh, yes. Splendid.

JANE. Now I've got to see these on. (*SHE hands him the Peter Cottontails.*)

SYBIL Jane!

JANE. Oh, relax Syb, it will only take a minute. Sebastian, would you mind taking the boxers off?

(*SEBASTIAN immediately starts to remove the boxers. PAUL sees this and heads for the French door. GEORGE grabs him to stop him. THEY struggle.*)

JANE. NOT HERE!! I mean, would you mind changing in the bathroom?

(*JANE shows SEBASTIAN into the bathroom and closes the door. PAUL breaks away from George, reaches the*

French door and opens it. GEORGE grabs him and pulls him away from the door, and slams it shut. BOTH of them immediately hide. Just as the WOMEN turn to see what caused the noise, the PHONE rings. SYBIL crosses to answer the phone while JANE collects the three men's outfits together.)

SYBIL. *(Answering phone.)* Hello? ... yes Suzanne ... What? ... You're kidding. *(Looks at her watch.)* How did it happen? .... Oh, no. What an idiot. I hope they find him, whoever he is ... Oh, poor you. Poor us! Right, well, thanks for phoning. We'll be in touch ... No, we'll figure something out. Not to worry. Hope you dry out soon . . yes. 'Bye. *(Hangs up.)* Oh, GOD! Catastrophe!

JANE. What?

SYBIL. That was Suzanne, calling from downstairs. Some clown threw a camera off his balcony just as she was coming in to the hotel and it knocked her into the swimming pool!

JANE. Oh, poor thing. Is she coming up?

SYBIL. No, she's a mess. She's going home to recover.

JANE. Oh no! What are we going to do?

SYBIL. I'm thinking, I'm thinking. Blast! We're running out of time!

JANE. Maybe we should call another agency.

SYBIL. We'd never be able to get someone this late in the day.

JANE. There must be someone we can call.

SYBIL. Who else do you know that has her measurements?

(SEBASTIAN enters from the bathroom, wearing the Peter Cottontails.)

SEBASTIAN. How do I look?

SYBIL. You've got them on backwards.

SEBASTIAN. Oops. Sorry. *(HE exits into the bathroom.)*

JANE. There has to be someone we can call.

SYBIL. No, it's too late.

JANE. What are we going to do then?

SYBIL. We'll have to model the women's line ourselves.

JANE. Are you nuts?

SYBIL. Do you have a better idea?

JANE. *(Picks a really skimpy pair of string bikini briefs out of a box.)* Do you seriously expect me to wear this in front of Fru Fru? It's too humiliating. I'm not going to do it. Forget it.

SYBIL. *(Tersely.)* Fine I'll do it.

JANE. You? What are you talking about? You've never modelled in your life.

SYBIL. Jane, we're talking about modelling, not brain surgery.

JANE. Syb, you know what I mean. Models know how to wear this sort of thing.

SYBIL. And I don't?

JANE. No, it's just that—it's not as easy as it looks

SYBIL. How hard can it be?

(SYBIL selects a teddy from the rack, begins to prance across the room, holding it in front of her, in bad imitation of a model. On the balcony, GEORGE's head

suddenly pops out from the edge of the French doors,
followed by PAUL's head below his The TWO
HUSBANDS watch the following scene, goggle-eyed)

SYBIL. (*Holding Teddy against herself.*) What do you
think? Is this too much?
JANE. No, it's perfect—if you're planning to appear on
America's Funniest Home Videos.

(JANE turns toward the French doors. GEORGE drags
PAUL behind cover.)

SYBIL Thanks a bunch. At least I was willing to try
JANE. Sorry Syb, but how can we expect Fru Fru to
take us seriously if you're negotiating contracts in your
knickers?
SYBIL. Well, it's too late to get a professional.
JANE. We can't parade around the room in our
underwear. We need someone who gets *paid* to parade
around the room in their underwear.
SYBIL. I guess we'll just have to display the women's
line on the rack.
JANE. That won't do. We want to show Fru Fru how
the male and female lines complement each other,
(*Holding up a female undergarment.*) and in order to do
that, we have to hang these on a body.
SYBIL. (*After a beat.*) Does it have to be a live body?
JANE. (*Suspiciously.*) What's the alternative?
SYBIL. Mannequins!
JANE. (*Relieved.*) Mannequins, of course! (*Pause.*)
Where are we going to find mannequins?

SYBIL. Downstairs. There have to be at least three clothing stores on the concourse level and they all have mannequins in the window. I'm sure that with my powers of persuasion, I can sweet-talk one of those store owners into lending us a couple for the afternoon.

JANE. (*Beat.*) Better take some cash.

SYBIL. Thank you. How much have you got?

(*The HUSBANDS reappear at the French doors and watch as the WOMEN rummage around in their purses. THEY each produce a wad of bills. The HUSBANDS exchange looks.*)

JANE. Here. Take it all.

SYBIL. (*Takes the money, kisses it.*) Please, God, let this work out. Come along, Jane Let's go dig up a couple of bodies.

(*SYBIL and JANE exit. PAUL and GEORGE enter from the balcony.*)

GEORGE. (*Examining the sleeve of his jacket.*) Damn pigeons!

PAUL. (*Pacing.*) Why did you stop me? We had them dead to rights! I was all set to come in here and put an end to this!

GEORGE. Put an end to what?

PAUL. To what's going on in here!

GEORGE. Paul, I know it all looks very suspicious, but I'm not convinced it's what you think it is.

PAUL. What would it take to convince you? A pair of horns growing out of your head?

GEORGE I know my wife. She simply would not do anything like this. Besides, as yet we haven't actually seen them do anything.

PAUL. Haven't seen them do anything? Are you blind? What about this? (*Imitating Jane's rubbing the briefs on her face.*) And this! (*Imitates Sybil's model walk.*) And THIS! (*Crosses to George, gets down on his knees, and grabs him by the buns.*)

(*At this very moment, the bathroom door opens, and SEBASTIAN walks in wearing the Peter Cottontails. HE takes to Paul and George.*)

SEBASTIAN. Excuse me.

(*PAUL and GEORGE shriek and leap away from each other as if electrocuted.*)

GEORGE. Where did you come from?
SEBASTIAN. The bathroom. I'll just be in here if you need me—

(*HE turns to go into the bathroom. GEORGE and PAUL chase him around the room.*)

PAUL and GEORGE. OH, NO YOU DON'T!

(*SEBASTIAN tries to get back to the bathroom. GEORGE gets there first and blocks the door. HE turns to escape, and runs into Paul. PAUL and GEORGE back him up and march him around the room.*)

PAUL. You're not going anywhere. We want to talk to you.

SEBASTIAN. Please, guys, this isn't my thing.

PAUL. (*Looking down at the Peter Cottontails*) You mean it's a prosthesis?

SEBASTIAN. No, no, I mean, I'm just not into it.

PAUL. Don't give me that. We know what you're into.

SEBASTIAN. (*Gulps.*) You do?

PAUL. What I want to know is, how much do you charge?

SEBASTIAN. Believe me, you couldn't pay me enough

PAUL You can't be more than the other one. He didn't even do anything, and he wanted three hundred bucks an hour

GEORGE. Plus parking.

SEBASTIAN I'm sorry, I really am. I'm sure you're very nice guys. I don't know who you are, or what you're doing here—well I mean, I *do* know what you're doing here—

PAUL. You don't understand—we need you.

SEBASTIAN. No, you don't. Believe me. What you need is—listen, I've got a friend. He won't charge you anything at all! He does it for fun! Tell you what—I'll just go and get him for you. (*HE bolts for the door and exits.*)

GEORGE. Gee, he even runs like a rabbit.

PAUL. He'll be rabbit stew if he shows that tail of his in here again. So, are you convinced yet?

GEORGE. I must admit, it doesn't look good ...

PAUL. George, you've just seen a guy running around your wife's hotel room wearing nothing but a pair of bunny ears! What more do you need?

GEORGE. I don't know—maybe we'll find out when the next guy shows up.

(The PHONE rings. GEORGE goes over and picks up the receiver.)

GEORGE. (*Very reasonable.*) Hello. . . No, she's not .. Who am I? George Brunt. Who are you? ... Cliff Strang.
PAUL. (*Holds up Cliff's photo and points to it.*) Cliff
GEORGE. (*To Paul.*) SSh!! ... And you're here for your 3 o'clock "session"?
PAUL. (*Grinding his hips, obscenely.*) Session
GEORGE. (*To Paul.*) Huh? ... (*Into the phone, still reasonable.*) Oh, sorry. What was that? . (*HE turns to Paul.*) He says he's so excited about this he can hardly contain himself ... (*Into phone.*) Yes, I see ... (*To Paul*) He says, this is virgin territory, and he can't wait to get started ... *because he's never done it in a hotel room before!*

(PAUL smiles in triumph and shrugs.)

GEORGE. (*Gathering steam.*) Well I've got some bad news for you, "Cliff," there isn't going to be any 3 o'clock "session" ... That's right. It's been postponed. Permanently ... That's right—no session. And no session fee, either ... I wouldn't come up here if I were you, Cliff—it might not be good for your health. No, I think you'd better just saddle up that goat of yours and ride on out of town. (*To Paul.*) He hung up.
PAUL. Now who's scaring them off?

GEORGE. What are you talking about?

PAUL (*Mimicking George.*) You should have let him come up—let them get on with it. Get it all on tape—

GEORGE. Little tricky now that the camera's decorating the parking lot. Besides I've seen all I need to see.

PAUL. Seeing isn't enough, I'm afraid. You said it yourself—we need some hard evidence.

GEORGE. (*Indicating the door.*) Bugs Bunny there was all the hard evidence we needed, and you let him hop out the door.

PAUL. Me? I was trying to interrogate him! What the hell were you doing?

GEORGE. Look, there's no point in crying over runaway rabbits. What's done is done.

PAUL. So what are we going to do now?

GEORGE. (*Crossing to the bedroom.*) I'll tell you what *I'm* going to do. I'm going to spoil their fun and games. I'm going to take their toys (*HE returns with several empty boxes and starts flinging stuff into them.*) and I'm going home. You're welcome to join me if you want.

PAUL. My God, what a little conviction does to a man! Maybe you're right. I don't think I'm cut out to be a voyeur.

GEORGE. Well then, don't just stand there—give me a hand.

PAUL. Right. (*HE grabs an empty box and begins to collect lingerie from the rack.*) I always wondered what their fascination was with the underwear business.

GEORGE. I'm more concerned about their fascination with the monkey business.

PAUL. It's so humiliating—to think that for three years we've been fooled into believing this was a legitimate enterprise, when all this time it was just a front for them to indulge their fantasies.

GEORGE. I had no idea Sybil's fantasies included goats. (*HE inspects a rather large-cup bra and puts it in his pocket.*)

PAUL And to think they have to pay for the privilege! It's so degrading!! Three hundred bucks an hour!

GEORGE. Plus parking.

PAUL. (*Looks around the room. THEY have cleaned out most of the hanging garments.*) Let's get this stuff down to the car. We'll have to come back for the rest (*THEY lift a box each.*)

GEORGE. What if security sees us with all this? Aren't we going to look somewhat suspicious?

PAUL. Good point. There's a fire exit at the other end of the hall. Let's take the stairs.

(*HE exits, carrying one of the boxes. GEORGE looks around the room and follows him.*)

GEORGE. (*From off.*) I'm leaving the door open—(*His voice fades.*) I don't want to wear out my blood donor card—

(*The tiniest of beats.*)

JANE. (*Off.*) Ow!
SYBIL. (*Off.*) What happened?
JANE. (*Off.*) The elevator tried to eat my foot!

(JANE and SYBIL enter the main door from the right, huffing and puffing, carrying a mannequin each.)

JANE. How could anything this thin weigh this much?
SYBIL. *(Putting down mannequin.)* Phew!
JANE. Did you leave the door open?
SYBIL. No. I thought you did.

(SHE looks around the room, looks back to mannequin, double-takes to missing lingerie, races into the bedroom to look, comes back in and SCREAMS. At the sound of Sybil's scream, JANE's head snaps up and collides with the mannequin SHE's attempting to put down DS.)

JANE. Ow!! What is it?
SYBIL. We've been robbed!!!
JANE. We've been robbed? *(Looks around the room, screams, looks at mannequin.)* WE'VE BEEN ROBBED!!

(JANE and SYBIL run around the room, panicking.)

JANE. What are we gonna do? What are we gonna do?
SYBIL. *(Running around the room, checking in empty boxes, behind cushions, under the couch, etc.)* I can't believe it! How could this happen? We've only been gone five minutes!
JANE. *(Running around in little circles, pacing back and forth.)* What are we gonna do? What are we gonna do?
SYBIL. *(Continuing her search.)* Who would want to steal a bunch of lingerie? *(SHE holds up a small pair of bikini briefs.)* Must be an anorexic theft ring or something.

JANE (*Running up to Sybil and grabbing her by the shoulders.*) What are we gonna do? What are we gonna do?

SYBIL. What are we gonna do? Fruferelli's going to be here any minute. I'll tell you what we're gonna do—we're gonna ... we're gonna ... we're gonna jump off the balcony, that's what we're gonna do!!

JANE. Good idea. (*Takes a step toward the balcony*)

SYBIL (*Yanking Jane back.*) Bad idea. Now, come on We're adults. We're intelligent. We're capable. We can figure a way out of this. Think!

JANE. But we're going to lose out on our five million bucks!!

SYBIL. THINK!!

(*THEY pace in step, JANE following SYBIL.*)

JANE. (*Thinks hard for a few seconds.*) I still like the balcony idea.

SYBIL. (*Ignoring her.*) I've got it! We'll call security!!

(*THEY both march to the phone, in step, and reach for the receiver.*)

SYBIL. Wait a moment—they're going to want details. Let's figure out what's missing.

(*THEY both head for the nearest empty box and peer into it in unison.*)

SYBIL (*Looks at Jane.*) You know, there's a better way of doing this. You figure out what's missing, I'll call security

JANE. Right

(*SYBIL dashes to the phone, JANE grabs Sybil's checklist and pen and starts making notes.*)

SYBIL. (*Into phone.*) Could you put me through to Security please? ... Hello, Security? This is room 504. I'd like to report a robbery ... Lingerie ... LINGERIE .. (*Sighs.*) L, I, N— (*Through gritted teeth.*) underwear ... That's right ... Oh, I don't know exactly, several dozen pieces, anyway ... Yes, it all belongs to me. Us. ... My friend. My business partner ... No, not that kind of business, the LINGERIE business! ... L, I, N—look, never mind, could you just send someone up here? Thank you. (*Hangs up phone.*) They're on their way.   ⌐

JANE. Good. (*Looking in boxes.*) It doesn't look as if they've taken any of the men's stuff—just what we need—transvestite burglars.

SYBIL. Sebastian!

JANE. What about him?

SYBIL. (*Heading for the bathroom.*) We left him in the bathroom.

JANE. (*Following her.*) Oh my God—do you think he did it?

(*As SYBIL and JANE disappear into the bathroom, PAUL enters through the main door wearing a huge sombrero tied with a string under his chin. GEORGE follows on his heels wearing a balaclava.*)

GEORGE. A little late for disguises, isn't it?
PAUL. You never know who you're going to run into.

(THEY begin throwing the rest of the lingerie in boxes.)

GEORGE. Couldn't we have picked something a little less conspicuous?
PAUL. That's all I had in the trunk.
GEORGE. Whatever you say, Sancho!
PAUL. Well, it looks like we've got most of it—*(Sees the bathroom door.)* what's in here?

(PAUL opens the bathroom door. HE and GEORGE disappear inside, closing the door behind themselves Brief pause, immediately followed by a loud SCREAM from EVERYONE in the bathroom. The door flies open, and GEORGE comes out with his hands up, followed by SYBIL, with a blow-dryer stuck pistol-fashion between his shoulder blades.)

GEORGE. Don't shoot! Don't shoot!
SYBIL. Hold it right there!

(GEORGE and SYBIL are immediately followed by JANE, dragging PAUL out of the room by the handle of a plunger which has been stuck to his face. Paul's sombrero is gone. JANE follows GEORGE and SYBIL to centre, swings PAUL around by the handle, and stops him centre stage. SHE plants a foot on his middle and pulls. The plunger comes off, revealing a large

*black ring on Paul's face. At the same time, SYBIL
grabs George's balaclava and pulls it off.)*

JANE. Paul!

SYBIL. George! What are you doing here? We thought
you were burglars!

GEORGE. *(To Sybil, looking at the blow dryer.)* Is that
thing loaded?

SYBIL. What? *(Looks down at dryer.)* Oh. Sorry.
(Tosses it away.) Anyway, you haven't answered my
question. What are you two doing here?

GEORGE. *(Smouldering.)* The same could be asked of
you.

SYBIL. What do you mean, darling?

GEORGE. Don't you "darling" me—

PAUL. *(Interrupting him.)* That's right, don't you
darling him—*(To George.)* what did I tell you? Number
one—pretend nothing is wrong. *(To Jane.)* We know
exactly what you're up to.

JANE. *(Confused.)* You do?

PAUL. Do I look like an idiot?

JANE. *(Looking at the black plunger ring on his face.)*
Well—

PAUL. Don't answer that. What I mean is, we'd have
to be idiots not to know what's going on here.

JANE. I have no idea what you're talking about.

PAUL *(To George.)* There we are—number two.
Denial.

JANE. Denial of what?

PAUL. Oh come on, Jane, the clues are all around
you—the hotel suite, *(Waves at photos)* the entertainment,

(*Indicates the boxes.*) and all these other "frills"—pulling out all the stops for Sybil's mum, aren't you?

JANE (*To Sybil.*) I told you that excuse was getting a little thin.

SYBIL (*To Jane.*) Be quiet. (*To George.*) How did you know where to find us?

GEORGE. Easy. We followed you.

SYBIL. You what?

JANE. (*To Paul.*) And you went along with this?

GEORGE. It was his idea ...

PAUL. Shut up.

GEORGE. ... even brought a video camera with him

PAUL. SHUT UP!!

SYBIL. You mean you broke in here?

GEORGE. Well, we didn't exactly "break" in. We slipped the lock with a blood donor card.

JANE. Ask a silly question!

PAUL. I'm calling my lawyer.

SYBIL. (*Outraged.*) You just might need him. (*To George.*) I don't know why you've done this, but you are about to screw up the most exciting afternoon of our lives—

GEORGE. Woman, have you no shame?

SYBIL. —and we have far too much to do without having to worry about the pair of you. But take my word for it, George Brunt, when I get you alone you're not going to know what hit you.

PAUL. Number Three. The attack.

SYBIL. (*Rounding on Paul.*) And don't think I don't know who started all this! When I'm finished with him I'm coming after you!

PAUL. She's bloody insatiable, George!

SYBIL. (*Pushing George.*) Now get out of my way. As if your arrival isn't catastrophic enough, we also have to deal with a robbery. Some pervert has ripped off most of our lingerie.

GEORGE. Must have been Harvey.

JANE. Who?

GEORGE. That six-foot rabbit you were keeping in the bathroom. We chased him out of here.

JANE. (*To Sybil.*) So it was Sebastian, after all.

GEORGE. (*Singing.*) "There goes Peter Cottontail, hoppin' down the bunny trail ..."

SYBIL. George! This is a crisis! You could at least show us a little support!

GEORGE. (*Pulls the bra from his pocket.*) Looks to me as if you've got all the support you need.

SYBIL. Where did you get that?

PAUL. Where do you think he got it? (*Indicating boxes.*) Out of one of those bins of iniquity. Right after you finished your Gypsy Rose Lee routine. (*HE imitates her earlier "model walk."*)

SYBIL. What are you doing?

GEORGE. Looks like the Funky Chicken to me

JANE. You took the stuff? You mean you broke in here and stole our lingerie? What gall, what unmitigated gall, Paul! How could you do something so stupid?

PAUL. I think we were very brave.

GEORGE. And I think we were totally justified.

JANE. And I think we'll have you both arrested! Do you realize what you've done?

PAUL. I think we have a pretty good idea

SYBIL You don't have a clue. You idiots! You may have cost us our future. We stood to make a lot of money here today.

GEORGE. Stood? And how much do you expect to make lying down?

SYBIL. George, what on earth has got into you?

GEORGE. The question is, what has got into YOU?

SYBIL. The thrill of private enterprise.

GEORGE. (*Pole-axed.*) Oh my God.

SYBIL. Look, we don't have time to stand around and argue. So you two can just go and retrieve the things you stole and bring them back here on the double.

PAUL. We'll do nothing of the kind. If you think we're going to be party to this "private enterprise" of yours, you're sadly mistaken. (*PAUL crosses his arms.*)

JANE. Fine. Where did you put them? We'll get them ourselves.

(*GEORGE imitates Paul's stance. THEY look at one another, then back to the women and shrug.*)

JANE. You listen to me, Paul. If you don't return our property immediately, we're calling the police.

GEORGE. You wouldn't dare.

SYBIL and JANE. Try us.

GEORGE. Come on, Paul, let's get the rest of these scanties out of here.

(*HE scoops up an armload. PAUL does likewise.*)

SYBIL. (*Running to the door and barring the way.*) Call the police, Jane, call the police.

(JANE runs to the phone and starts dialling furiously.)

PAUL. You'll thank us for this one day.

(The MEN turn to leave. There is a KNOCK at the door. JANE looks at the receiver.)

SYBIL. Who is it?
HODGE. *(Off.)* It's Security, ma'am.
GEORGE. *(To Paul.)* That was quick.
SYBIL. *(Opens the door.)* Thank God you're here! The burglars are back. *(Points to Paul and George.)* There they are—arrest them!

(HODGE starts toward PAUL and GEORGE, who back off.)

PAUL. This isn't what it looks like. We're not burglars—we're their husbands.
HODGE. *(Advances toward them. HE has squeaky shoes.)* That's a new one.
GEORGE. It's true! We're just having a little domestic dispute, that's all.
HODGE. Looks more like fun and games to me. Now are you two going to come quietly, or am I going to have to get nasty?
PAUL Look, you've got it all wrong—I'm no crook, I'm a lawyer!
HODGE There's a contradiction if ever I heard one! *(HE grabs Paul and George by the scruff of the neck and*

holds them up.) What do you say, ladies? Are these two men your husbands, or aren't they?

(SYBIL and JANE look at one another, then back to Hodge)

SYBIL. Never seen them before in our lives.

(HODGE begins to frog-march PAUL and GEORGE toward the door. THEY ad-lib to their wives as the LIGHTS fade.)

END OF ACT I

ACT II

*Same scene as Act I. The room has been cleaned up and
readied for Fruferelli's arrival. The mannequins are set
up DR dressed in various pieces of lingerie with wigs,
shoes, etc. The wigs on the mannequins should be very
similar in color to Sybil and Jane's hair. They look
great. There are extra wigs in an open box beside the
screen. The boxes of lingerie that Paul and George
removed in Act I are back in the room. Outfits are
hanging on the outer part of the screen. The champagne
has been delivered. It stands in an ice bucket with
glasses around it. The models' photos have been
removed. A beat. On the balcony a line of sheets, tied
together, drops down from above. Another beat. Then a
pair of feet appears, dangling from above. Slowly, the
owner of the feet makes his way down the line of sheets
It's PAUL. HE is looking distinctly dishevelled. HE
descends to the balcony and goes through an elaborate,
military-style maneuver to see that the coast is clear
inside the room. HE sees the two mannequins standing
in the room and assumes they are Jane and Sybil,
dressed for action. HE nods in satisfaction, then looks
up the line of sheets and beckons. Beat. Another pair of
feet appears swinging back and forth. It's GEORGE.
HE also looks very much the worse for wear. We hear a
huge, RIPPING SOUND and GEORGE swings right by
the window. HE disappears off SL with a SCREAM.
There is a CRASH offstage. PAUL, horrified, rushes to*

*the edge of the balcony and looks over. As HE scans
below for signs of George's mangled corpse, GEORGE
enters from the bedroom, the bedroom curtain wrapped
around him like a toga. HE spots the mannequins,
thinks they are the women, creeps out onto the balcony
and closes the doors. HE walks up to Paul who is still
looking below, trying to find George. GEORGE looks
down as well, trying to see what Paul is looking for
PAUL looks up, sees George, and looks back down
again. HE immediately double-takes to George, and
freaks out. GEORGE, frightened by Paul's response,
does the same. THEY hug each other in relief.
GEORGE indicates the two mannequins to Paul, who
nods his understanding. The TWO of them enter the
room boldly. N.B. The above action takes place in
mime.*

PAUL. Surprise, surprise. We're back.
GEORGE. And don't think it was easy, either. That
security guard is going to be awfully upset when he wakes
up.
PAUL. So get your coats. We're leaving.

*(GEORGE takes the mannequin he has mistaken for Sybil
by the hand and attempts to lead her toward the door.
The hand comes off in his. GEORGE screams and
drops it.)*

PAUL. That was very deft.
GEORGE. (*Picking up the hand.*) Actually, it's her
right.

PAUL. What the hell are these dummies doing here anyway?

GEORGE. (*Trying to re-attach the hand.*) Refusing to co-operate, for one thing

PAUL Here, let me give you a hand!

(With a look to Paul, GEORGE gives him the hand. PAUL attempts to re-attach it)

GEORGE. (*Rubbing his shoulder.*) Were all those acrobatics really necessary?

PAUL. It's all I could think of. I saw that pile of sheets on the maid's cart and the idea came to me

GEORGE I still don't understand why we had to come back. I mean, after the incident in the kitchen we could have taken off and headed for the hills.

PAUL And leave Sybil and Jane alone here to do as they please? Not on your life (*HE succeeds in re-attaching the hand.*) Anyway, I wasn't the only one indulging in acrobatics. What about that stunt you pulled on our friend from Security?

GEORGE. Well, it serves old Hodge right for frog-marching us through the kitchen like that

PAUL Why the hell did you have to shove him into that dessert trolley?

GEORGE I didn't "shove" him. It was an accident. I tripped over a crouton.

PAUL. And knocked him face-first into the profiteroles.

GEORGE. They must have been stale. Knocked him out cold.

(There is a KNOCK at the door. PAUL and GEORGE freeze)

GEORGE. *(Whispering.)* Who can that be?
PAUL. It can't be our wives, they wouldn't knock
GEORGE. It can't be one of the pretty boys—we've scared them all away
PAUL. Maybe it's the goat.

(There is another KNOCK.)

GEORGE. *(In falsetto.)* Who is it?

(PAUL stares at George in horror. GEORGE shrugs.)

HODGE. Security, ma'am. Please open up.
PAUL and GEORGE. HODGE!
GEORGE. He woke up
PAUL. And if he finds us, we're toast. Come on. *(HE heads for the bedroom.)*
GEORGE. Come on where? We can't start hiding now. He knows we're in here!
PAUL. What do you suggest we do then?
GEORGE. How am I supposed to know?

(There is another KNOCK at the door.)

PAUL. *(To George.)* Say something!
GEORGE. *(In a Dame Edith Evans falsetto.)* Just a minute—we're not decent.

HODGE I really must insist that you open this door, Ma'am.

GEORGE. (*Falsetto.*) Just a moment please! (*GEORGE thrusts a Merry Widow and chemise at Paul and pushes him toward the screen.* Whispering.) Put that on.

PAUL. (*Thrusts it back at George.*) You've got to be kidding.

GEORGE You have a better idea?

PAUL. Um—

GEORGE. Right. Here.

(GEORGE hands PAUL the lingerie again. PAUL goes behind the screen. GEORGE finds a two-piece negligee and a pair of mule slippers. HE tears off his clothes and begins to put on the negligee. NB—as Paul undresses, HE throws his clothes over the edge of the screen so that they are visible to the audience. HE should be underdressed as much as possible.)

GEORGE. (*Falsetto.*) Yes, sir. What can I do for you?

HODGE. It's strictly a routine matter, Ma'am I'm investigating a disturbance. Have you noticed anything unusual?

GEORGE. (*Falsetto.*) No, sir. It's all quiet in here.

HODGE. Well, ma'am, I have to check it out for myself. Could you let me in, please?

GEORGE. (*Falsetto.*) It's not very convenient at the moment.

HODGE. It's for your own security, ma'am. Please open the door.

GEORGE. We're very busy right now.

HODGE. It won't take a minute, ma'am.

(GEORGE looks for and finds some lipstick, and applies it to his cheeks and lips.)

GEORGE. *(Falsetto.)* Uh—alright. I'll be right there. *(HE checks himself in the mirror. Own voice.)* There's something wrong with this picture. *(Falsetto.)* Just let me throw something on

(HE looks around in a hurry, spots the wig box open by the screen, takes out a wig, dumps it on his head, and throws another one over the screen to Paul. PAUL squeals.)

GEORGE. Put that on! *(GEORGE goes to the door and opens it. Falsetto.)* Sorry to keep you waiting.

(HODGE enters, plodding through the room, giving it a cursory check—under the couch, etc. GEORGE follows him.)

HODGE. That's alright—*(Taking George in.)* uh, ma'am. You're not Mrs. Brunt.
GEORGE. *(Falsetto.)* No, but close—er—close friends of hers.
HODGE Sorry for the inconvenience, ma'am. Those two thieves have escaped, and were spotted climbing up the side of the building. Have you seen or heard anything out of the ordinary?
GEORGE. *(As HE see a piece of Paul's clothing flop over the top of the screen.)* No, not a thing.

HODGE. (*Checking the bathroom.*) What's all this in here? (*HODGE disappears into the bathroom.*)

GEORGE. (*Falsetto*) Oh, nothing. We were just— doing a little laundry. (*GEORGE picks up his clothes from the floor.*)

HODGE. (*Re-entering.*) I've locked the window for your protection. Now I'd just like to check the bedroom.

(HE exits into the bedroom. GEORGE crosses to the telephone table and hurls his clothes underneath it. HE looks at the fruit bowl on the table, takes a couple of apples out and stuffs them in his bra. HE then notices Paul's clothes over the edge of the screen and grabs them. HE bundles them up into a ball and is about to chuck them onto the balcony when HODGE returns. HE hides them behind his back. HODGE crosses to George.)

HODGE. I notice you've had a little trouble with your window. Are you quite sure you haven't heard anything?

GEORGE. No, not a dickey-bird.

HODGE. Right. Well, I'll just have a look on the balcony.

(HE exits. GEORGE moves toward the bedroom to get rid of Paul's clothes, but HODGE re-enters before he makes it. GEORGE hides them behind his back again.)

HODGE. All's ... (*Takes to George's new chest.*) well out there, ma'am.

GEORGE. (*Falsetto.*) Good. (*HE is looking for some way of getting rid of Paul's clothes.*)

HODGE. I'll just take a peek behind here, and then I'll be off.

(HODGE makes his way toward the screen. GEORGE goes as if to stop him, but as HODGE steps behind the screen, PAUL comes out the other end. HE looks great. Merry Widow, stockings, garter belt, wig, false eyelashes and high-heel shoes. HE stumbles a little, crossing to the couch. HE does a male adjustment to his crotch as HODGE comes out from behind the screen.)

HODGE. *(Looks appreciatively at Paul.)* Well well, where have you been hiding yourself, little lady?

PAUL. *(Sexy falsetto.)* Somewhere you'd never think to look, Big Boy.

GEORGE. *(Falsetto.)* I think I need some air. *(HE rushes to the French doors, goes out on the balcony and flings Paul's clothes over the edge. HE takes a couple of deep breaths, adjusts his wig and re-enters.)*

HODGE. That's quite an outfit you have on. You and your friends must be planning a party.

PAUL. *(Falsetto.)* Friends?

HODGE. Mrs. Brunt and Mrs. Pritchard. You are friends of theirs, aren't you?

PAUL. *(Falsetto.)* Er—yes. Something like that.

HODGE. I take it they've gone out. Left you in charge, have they?

PAUL. *(Falsetto.)* Yes, that's right, they'll be back soon. They've just gone to do a little—*(Looks down, sees George's fishing vest on the floor. HE gives it a discreet kick under the couch.)* fishing.

HODGE Fishing?

GEORGE. (*In falsetto.*) Thank you so much for looking out for us, Mr —

HODGE. Hodge. (*To Paul.*) But my friends call me Rodge.

PAUL. (*Falsetto.*) Why would they want to do that?

HODGE. Because it's my name. Roger Hodge.

GEORGE. (*Falsetto.*) Your parents should be flodged—I mean flogged. Anyway, thanks for all your relp, Hodge—I mean help, Rodge.

PAUL. (*Falsetto.*) Let me show you out.

(HODGE watches PAUL cross in front of him. HE pinches Paul's rear end. PAUL yelps, gives him a fierce look. HE opens the door.)

HODGE. I'll be back. (*HE gives Paul a huge wink.*)

PAUL. Sure. (*HE winks back. His eyelash sticks shut. The wink seems to go on forever.*)

(HODGE gives a dirty laugh and exits, nodding politely to George. PAUL closes the door.)

GEORGE. (*Taking out his apples.*) Well, that didn't go too badly.

PAUL. Did you see that pinch? I won't be able to sit down for a week!

GEORGE. Yes, it's awful when men treat you like an object, isn't it?

PAUL. And what do they use to get these damn false eyelashes off? Paint thinner? I can't get unstuck.

GEORGE. Here, I'll help you.

(GEORGE attempts to pull off Paul's false eyelash. PAUL yelps.)

PAUL. I think I'd have preferred the paint thinner. *(Goes to mirror.)* God—I look like Captain Hook in drag. All I need is a parrot.

GEORGE. It worked, didn't it? We got rid of him, at least.

PAUL. For the time being. What do I do when he comes back?

GEORGE. He'll never recognize you—you'll be a man again!

PAUL. Yeah—just the man he's looking for. I'm either the burglar he can't wait to arrest or the woman he can't wait to seduce. *(Looks George up and down.)* If only I looked like you.

GEORGE. I take exception to that. I think I'm a very passable woman.

PAUL. Yes, he passed right by you.

GEORGE. You had more time to fix your face Besides, look what I had to wear.

PAUL. It's a poor workman who blames his tools.

GEORGE. Don't spout clichés at me. You even had a chance to do your eyelashes.

PAUL. It wasn't my eyelashes he was looking at.

GEORGE. At least you had something else for him to look at. *(Holding out apples.)* My boobs didn't pop up until halfway through!

PAUL. (*Taking an apple and beginning to eat it.*) Don't blame me. You're the one who wanted to dress up in women's clothes

GEORGE. (*Taking apple*) Give me that! I might need these again.

PAUL. You could always use an orange.

GEORGE. What do I look like—a fruit salad?

PAUL. If the shoe fits. ...

GEORGE. Oh, very nice. This is the thanks I get for saving our butts—

PAUL. (*Rubbing his behind.*) Speak for yourself. Another visit from Rodge and mine's going to end up in a sling. Look at me! This morning I was a successful divorce lawyer; and now, thanks to you, I'm a cheap harlot trying to dodge Rodge Hodge the randy hotel dick, who in my other life wants to arrest me for stealing ladies' underwear.

GEORGE. Lingerie.

PAUL. Shut up!

GEORGE (*Removes his wig.*) Well, I don't know about you, but I'm up for a sex change. I say we get out of these clothes and get the hell out of here. (*Sarcastically.*) Of course, if you have a *better* idea—

PAUL. I don't. Let's go.

(*HE starts to go towards the screen when we hear VOICES and LAUGHTER coming from the hallway. It is the WOMEN with FRU FRU.*)

GEORGE. They're back already—and I'm not dressed!

(*PAUL and GEORGE freeze. Beat. GEORGE suddenly dives for his clothes under the small table, looks toward*

the bedroom, realizes he isn't going to make it, and
hides under the table. PAUL races around for
inspiration, runs into one of the mannequins. As the
door opens, PAUL strikes a pose, his back to the door
SYBIL and JANE enter with FRU FRU.)

SYBIL. (*Ushering Fru Fru in.*) After you, Signor
Fruferelli. Let me get you a glass of champagne

(JANE pours the champagne. SYBIL helps FRU FRU off
with his coat. HE hangs his hat on Paul's hand.)

FRU FRU. Oh—Dom Perignon 1971! The same-a wine
you gave me een-a the leemo! (*JANE looks at SYBIL who*
shrugs.) You are trying to spoil me, no?
SYBIL. We just wanted to make you feel at home.
After all, you've gone to a lot of trouble on our behalf.
FRU FRU. I think maybe I 'ave 'ad enough.

(JANE gives him a drink. HE takes it without hesitation.)

FRU FRU. Maybe just one-a more. Salute. (*HE sips the*
champagne.) Magnifico!
SYBIL. Won't you sit down, Signor Fruferelli?
FRU FRU. Thank-a you. (*HE does.*) Eet eesa so gooda
to seet down, at last. Thees eesa the third country I 'ave-a
been in today. I theenk I'm-a feeling a beet of-a jet sag.
JANE Lag.
FRU FRU. *Si*, lag. Thank-a you. (*Takes another sip.*)
But thees, she make-a me forget my lag (*Looking around*

the room.) Ah, thees ees-a so nice. To be in a beautiful room, with a beautiful wine, and-a two beautiful ladies.

JANE. Thank you, Signor, but the pleasure is ours.

FRU FRU. *(Setting down his glass, looking at his watch.)* You are-a too kind. But asa they say, time and tide, she waita for no one, and I do 'ave a plane-a to catch, so— letta me see your goodies!

(Hearing this, PAUL lets out a strangled GASP and strains to see what's going on behind him. JANE and SYBIL glance around briefly for the source of the noise.)

SYBIL. Yes. Right. Well, to begin with, Signor, we'd like to show you swatches of some of the fabrics we didn't have with us at the trade show. *(SHE fetches a big binder.)* These are samples of the various colors we work in at present.

(SYBIL hands the binder to FRUFERELLI. HE examines the fabrics and fact sheets.)

FRU FRU. Mmmm. What do you call deesa color?

SYBIL. Scheherezade.

FRU FRU. Eetsa beautiful. Very unusual. *(Picks up fact sheet.)* Tell me, Senora Brunt, 'ow do you keepa your labor cost so low?

SYBIL. Oh, that's a little trade secret of ours. Her name's Lorraine.

FRU FRU. You mean one-a woman she make all ofa your designs?

SYBIL. Not entirely, but we'd be lost without her. She's very gifted.

FRU FRU. Well, maybe you geeve her to me for a geeft?

(FRU FRU laughs. SYBIL dutifully joins in.)

SYBIL. More champagne Signor?
FRU FRU. Eef-a you eenseest.

(HE holds out his glass and SYBIL fills it.
Meanwhile, as the above conversation takes place, JANE crosses to the rack to collect some samples. SHE passes Paul without noticing him. SHE selects a pile of lingerie, and crosses back in front of Paul. HE hisses at her. SHE stops, wondering what she's heard, and takes another step. PAUL hisses louder. SHE looks behind the screen. SHE crosses back, and HE hisses again. JANE turns around very slowly and suspiciously and comes into eye contact with Paul, who from his mannequin pose beckons to her sharply. JANE shrieks and drops the samples. SYBIL and FRU FRU turn to her in surprise.)

SYBIL. What's wrong?
JANE. Sorry?
SYBIL. You screamed.
JANE. Did I?
FRU FRU. Si, si. You say, "AAAAGH!"
JANE. Aaaaaah, yes. That. I tripped. Dropped my samples. Aah-ha. Ha ha ha.
FRU FRU. Oh, dear. Let-a me help-a you.

(FRU FRU gets up and starts to pick up samples from the floor. His head is down throughout the following. PAUL takes the opportunity to dash behind the screen to retrieve his clothes.)

SYBIL. Are you alright, Jane?
JANE. *(Vigorously shaking her head "no.")* Yes.
SYBIL. Huh?
JANE. *(Gesturing behind herself.)* I'm fine.
SYBIL. What are you doing?
JANE. *(In a fierce whisper.)* Can't you see—

(SHE turns around to look at where she thinks Paul should be and SCREAMS. FRU FRU, who has begun to stand up with his arms full of samples, is startled. HE shrieks and drops the lingerie. PAUL's hands appear at the top of the screen, feeling for his clothes.)

FRU FRU. What is it? What is-a wrong?
SYBIL. Nothing, Signor Fruferelli. Please, sit down. *(FRU FRU obliges.)* You must forgive us. We had a robbery earlier today, and my partner is a little nervous. Jane, how about some champagne?
JANE. Certainly. *(Takes Fru Fru's glass and downs it in a gulp.)*
SYBIL. For our *guest*, Jane.
JANE. Of course.

(JANE fills Fru Fru's glass. PAUL comes out from behind the screen, frantically looking for his clothes. HE spots the pile of lingerie on the floor, crosses to it, picks it up and starts to look through it)

FRU FRU. (*To Jane.*) Thank-a you. I think I need it. My heart, she is-a, how do you say, "humping."

SYBIL. I beg your pardon?

FRU FRU. Thumping.

SYBIL. Ah. I'm terribly sorry. Now, I know you're pressed for time, and I don't want to keep you any longer than necessary, so let me show you some of our new samples. (*Crossing to the spot where she last saw the lingerie. As she does so, PAUL freezes.*) These are the items from our male line that we showed you sketches of last week. We've chosen these fabrics specifically to complement our women's lines.

(SYBIL turns to pick up samples. PAUL hands them to her. SYBIL takes them.)

SYBIL. (*To Paul.*) Thank you.

(SYBIL double-takes to Paul. SHE prepares to scream. PAUL clamps a hand over her mouth. A MUFFLED SCREAM escapes. As FRU FRU looks up at the sound, SYBIL polishes his hand to cover, and twists him into another position.)

FRU FRU. Ladies, eef-a you will excuse-a me, I have-a to veezit the leetle boys.

SYBIL. (*Beat.*) Pardon?

FRU FRU. The leetle boys—(*Confidentially.*) you know.

FRU FRU. The leetle boys—in the leetle room.

SYBIL. Oh, the little boys room. How silly of us. Of course, Signor, it's right over here.

(FRU FRU gets up and crosses toward Sybil SYBIL takes him by the hand and leads him toward the bathroom. As THEY pass Paul, PAUL coughs. FRU FRU stops in his tracks and turns to Paul. JANE coughs a few times in an effort to cover it up. FRU FRU examines Paul closely.)

FRU FRU. A very unusual doll, this. Eencredible. So lifelike, no? *(Pats Paul's bum.)* Hmmm. *(Feels it in earnest.)* She even-a feels real.

(SYBIL tries to pull FRUFERELLI away. HE turns and goes with her for a step or so, during which PAUL, furious, grabs the bottle from Jane and goes after him. JANE holds him back. FRU FRU suddenly stops and looks back at Paul, and HE freezes. JANE laughs.)

FRU FRU. Huh! For a moment, I could-a swear she was-a breathing.

(HE laughs and turns away again. PAUL releases his breath and holds the bottle up as if to smash it on Fru Fru's head. FRU FRU turns around again. PAUL freezes. FRU FRU stares at Paul for a moment, then laughs it off.)

FRU FRU. It must-a be all thees-a champagne!

*(HE crosses toward the bathroom. JANE pulls PAUL back,
grabbing him under the arms. FRU FRU stops and
turns again. PAUL freezes once more.)*

FRU FRU. I must-a 'ave another look at thees-a doll.
She ees-a remarkable.

*(FRU FRU exits into the bathroom. JANE wheels on Paul,
who tries to get to the main door.)*

JANE. I don't know how you got back in here, or what
you're doing in that outfit, but I've got news for you—
you're staying like that.
PAUL. You've got to be kidding.
JANE. I'm not kidding. You have no idea what's at
stake here. You are jeopardizing a deal that could make us
very rich.
PAUL. Rich? How rich?
SYBIL. Five million dollars rich.
GEORGE. *(Leaps out from under the table, holding his
clothes. HE is still in full drag, minus one of the apples.)*
Five million dollars!
JANE and SYBIL. AAAGH!!!
SYBIL. What were you doing under there?
GEORGE. *(Taking a bite of apple.)* Having lunch!
PAUL. Now wait a minute. You mean to tell me that
guy's going to pay you five million bucks for a bunch of
underwear?
SYBIL. *(Through gritted teeth.)* Lingerie.
JANE. We're selling him the rights to our designs! He's
going to produce Passion Fashion Wear world-wide!

PAUL. Five million dollars.

SYBIL. That's right IF we can convince him to close the deal.

PAUL. Well, that's great. I'm behind you all the way I'll even draw up the contract for you—free of charge. (*Looks at his watch.*) But I'm afraid you'll have to do your convincing without me.

JANE. What are you talking about?

PAUL. I'm getting out of here.

SYBIL. Paul, please! You must stay! We need you!

PAUL. Forget it. I'm going.

JANE. (*Crosses to phone.*) You stay or I'm calling Security.

PAUL. Go ahead. Anything's better than getting felt up by Casanova. (*Beat.*) With the possible exception of getting felt up by Hodge. ...

JANE. You can't leave! Fruferelli has seen you! He's even taken a fancy to you.

PAUL. That's precisely my point. I want to make my getaway before he proposes I'm leaving, and no one's going to stop me.

GEORGE. (*Racing to the door and barring the exit.*) Hold it right there!

(*SYBIL cracks up.*)

GEORGE. What's so funny?

SYBIL. You look like a stand-in for Benny Hill.

GEORGE. Well it doesn't matter. My days as a woman are over. (*To Paul.*) Yours, on the other hand, are not.

PAUL. What do you mean?

GEORGE. You're going to do exactly what you're told, my friend. If it weren't for you and your silly suspicions, we wouldn't be in this mess in the first place. We're going to do whatever it takes to make this deal happen.

JANE. (*To Paul.*) And if it means you staying in that outfit for *three weeks,* you're going to do it.

SYBIL. Good I'm glad that's settled. Now do us a favor, darling, and disappear before we have to explain you to Fruferelli.

GEORGE. (*Looking down at his outfit.*) Good idea. (*Handing PAUL the apple.*) Here, hold this.

PAUL. What are you doing?

GEORGE. (*Shaking out his trousers.*) I'm getting dressed.

(*PAUL dives toward him. GEORGE whips the trousers away toreador style.*)

PAUL. Gimme those clothes!

GEORGE. Get your own. (*HE starts to get into the trousers.*)

PAUL. Where are they?

GEORGE. In the swimming pool, I think.

PAUL. What?

GEORGE. I threw them out the window.

PAUL. You WHAT? Gimme those clothes!

(*PAUL chases GEORGE around the room. GEORGE hops around the room, one leg in.*)

JANE. (*Jumping on his back.*) Don't do this, Paul We need you!

PAUL. Oh, get off my back.

SYBIL. (*Opening the bedroom door and beckoning.*) Quick, George, in here!

(GEORGE heads for the bedroom. PAUL shakes Jane off and blocks his path.)

PAUL. Oh no you don't.

GEORGE. (*Trying to muscle past Paul, still with only one leg in.*) Get out of the way, you harlot!

PAUL. George, it's my only hope. I've got to get into your pants!

GEORGE. (*Fluffing his hair.*) I bet you say that to all the boys.

(PAUL grabs the free pant leg and pulls. GEORGE struggles. JANE holds PAUL around the waist and tries to pull him away. A tug of war ensues. SYBIL attempts to get GEORGE into the bedroom. JANE opens the main door. Just as the bathroom door opens. SYBIL grabs GEORGE and throws him and his clothes out of the main door. PAUL freezes in his mannequin pose. FRU FRU enters, carrying several men's briefs. SYBIL closes the main door, JANE closes the bedroom door and FRU FRU closes the bathroom door simultaneously. HE crosses in. As HE passes Paul, HE stops.)

FRU FRU. Amazing. So life-a like.

(HE reaches up to touch Paul's face. SYBIL dives in to intercept, thrusting a glass of champagne into Fru Fru's hand)

SYBIL. Your champagne, Signor.

FRU FRU. Thank-a you.

SYBIL. *(Indicating the briefs as SHE turns away from Paul.)* Oh, I see you found some of our samples.

FRU FRU. Yes, I 'ope-a you don' mind, but I couldn't reseest—thees eesa your male line, yes?

SYBIL. Uh, some of it, yes.

FRU FRU. Bravissimo! *(Holds up a pair of boxer shorts.)* Such eenvention! Such-a innovation! Een-a Europe, they weel sell-a like-a pancakes! *(PAUL reacts.)* I'm-a so looking forward to seeing these ona the body. Where are your-a models?

(SYBil and JANE exchange horrified looks.)

JANE. *(Looks at her watch.)* Oh, my God!

SYBIL. They should be here any minute. In fact, one of them was here just a few minutes ago.

FRU FRU. Where did he go?

SYBIL. I don't know—he seems to have disappeared.

FRU FRU. *(A touch exasperated.)* Ees-a always the same with-a these models. Even een-a Milano! So unreliable. Never on-a the clock. *(Holds one of the samples up to Paul.)* Maybe we should-a put these on your-a doll here.

(JANE crosses to Fru Fru in order to guide him away from Paul FRU FRU looks at him closely.)

FRU FRU. But no, that would not-a work. After all, thees ees-a men's wear, and she ees-a very feminine, no? *(HE tweaks both of Paul's boobs, makes a sound like a train whistle.)* Wooo wooo!!

(FRU FRU turns around, laughing. The WOMEN laugh politely in response Then PAUL does precisely the same thing to Fru Fru's behind—train whistle and all. JANE jumps in front of Paul to stop him. FRU FRU wheels around, and sees Jane standing there, hands outstretched. HE assumes she's done it. JANE smiles at him.

JANE. *(Weakly.)* Wooo wooo!!

(FRU FRU smiles and winks at Jane. SYBIL attempts to rescue Jane by leading FRU FRU back towards the couch.)

SYBIL. Some more champagne, Signor Fruferelli?
FRU FRU. Eef-a you will join me, ladies.
JANE. *(Looks to Paul as if to say "Thanks a lot," then turns and smiles at Fru Fru.)* Why, of course, Signor Fruferelli.
FRU FRU. *(As HE pats the seat beside him.)* Please Call-a me Bruno.
JANE. *(Uncertainly.)* Bruno

(JANE sits, accepts the champagne from SYBIL and THEY ALL clink glasses.)

FRU FRU. Now. Where were we? (*HE looks at his watch and sees the men's briefs still in his hand.*) Oh yes—where are-a these-a models?
SYBIL. Uhhh—

(There is a KNOCK at the door.)

FRU FRU. Perhaps that is-a one of them now!

(SYBIL crosses to the door, opens it, GEORGE's head pops in. SHE slams the door in his face.)

SYBIL. Oooops! Wrong room!

(There is another, more urgent KNOCK on the door. SYBIL opens it a crack.)

SYBIL. (*Sotto voce.*) Go away.
GEORGE. (*Appearing in the doorway.*) Let me in! Hodge is coming down the hall!

(SHE shuts the door and turns and smiles at Fru Fru. Beat. There is a third, thunderously LOUD KNOCK on the door. It shakes in its frame. SYBIL ignores it and smiles nonchalantly. FRU FRU looks at Jane, obviously confused.)

JANE. (*Crosses to the door and opens it.*) Sybil, I think we should let *our model* in, don't you?

SYBIL. Our model. Oh, our model!

(*SYBIL opens the door. GEORGE bursts into the room and slams the door shut. HE is obviously distraught, and still carrying the lingerie he's just taken off. HE double-takes at seeing Fru Fru.*)

JANE. Where have you been? We've been waiting for you.

SYBIL. Yes, you've been a naughty boy, Geor— Giorgio.

GEORGE. *Who*?

FRU FRU. (*In Italian.*) Giorgio? You're Italian? What a wonderful surprise! *[Giorgio? Sei Italiano? Ma, che bella sorpresa!]*

(*GEORGE nods and smiles, casts a panicky look at Sybil.*)

FRU FRU. (*Italian.*) What's the matter? You're in such a state! And what's with the women's lingerie—did you get chased out of some bedroom by a jealous husband? *[Che cosa hai? Che sei cosi preoccupato? E con queste mutandine in mano? Ah! Sei scapato, eh? Scapato de qualche camera da letto e del marito che ti dava caccia.]*

GEORGE. (*Totally lost, looking from Fru Fru to Sybil and back again.*) Si, si.

FRU FRU. (*Italian.*) You're kidding! Good for you! (*Gives George a hug, kisses him.*) A man after my own heart! *[Scherzi? Bravo! Complimenti! Compagno mio!]*

(FRU FRU laughs heartily. GEORGE joins him, relieved that he's apparently said the right thing.)

SYBIL. Well, now that you two have had a chance to get acquainted, we should get down to business.

FRU FRU. Of course.

(There is a strange, beeper-like RINGING sound.)

JANE. What in the world is that?

FRU FRU. Oh, she's-a my telephone. (*HE takes a cellular phone out of his jacket pocket.*) Si? ... Si—one moment—ladies, thees ees-a a very eemportant call. I weel take it on-a de balcony, OK?

JANE. OK. I mean, of course, Signor Fruferelli. We'll get everything set up for you.

FRU FRU. Thees won't take-a long.

(FRU FRU bows and exits out on to the balcony. Beat. PAUL collapses out of his pose with a groan.)

GEORGE. Who the hell is Giorgio? His long lost brother?

SYBIL. No, our long lost model. At least, that's what Fruferelli thinks. And since there's no sign of Peter or Cliff, and Sebastian seems to have fallen off the edge of the earth, you'll have to do, Giorgio.

GEORGE. Do what, exactly?

SYBIL. Model our men's line, of course.

GEORGE. (*Holding up a skimpy pair of briefs.*) You want me to prance around the room in *this*?

SYBIL. You listen to me, George Brunt Once this deal is signed—if it's signed—you two will have a lot of explaining to do But if you don't want to blow our chance at the biggest deal of our lives, you're going to do exactly as I say.

PAUL. We're going to do whatever it takes to make this deal happen, remember?

SYBIL. (*To Paul.*) Thank you. (*Grabbing briefs from George's hand.*) And that means you are going to prance around in this! So hop to it, Giorgio!

GEORGE. Forget it (*HE heads for the door.*)

SYBIL. Where do you think you're going?

GEORGE. Back to the old country. (*GEORGE opens the door and immediately slams it shut*)

SYBIL. What's the matter?

GEORGE. It's Hodge! He's in the hallway!

SYBIL. So you're staying. How magnanimous of you (*SHE scoops up some male garments and thrusts them at him.*) Start with this, followed by these, and this. That should do it. And do try to hold your stomach in, dear.

GEORGE. Give me one good reason why I should do this.

SYBIL. (*Calling.*) Mr. Hodge!

GEORGE. That'll do.

SYBIL. Good. (*SHE pushes him behind the screen.*) I'll help you.

(*THEY go. PAUL groans. JANE goes to him.*)

PAUL. (*Opens a garter, rolls down a stocking and scratches his thigh.*) I can't stay here. I can't. Let me go. PLEEEEEEASE! Now's my chance!

JANE. No way. You're staying.

PAUL. I may never walk again. (*Looks down.*) I may never do anything again.

JANE. Tough titty.

PAUL. You can say that again. (*HE rearranges his bosom.*)

JANE. You can't leave Fru Fru's fascinated by you.

PAUL. I'll keel over if I have to stand like that any longer.

JANE. Then pick an easier pose.

PAUL. (*Sits on the arm of the chair.*) How about this?

JANE. (*Pulling him up.*) Don't be ridiculous.

(*SHE starts to roll up his stocking. PAUL gets the giggles and starts jiggling.*)

JANE. Hold still!

PAUL. Ooooh, that tickles!

(*HE giggles audibly as FRU FRU enters.*)

FRU FRU. Sorry to keep-a you waiting—

(*PAUL and JANE freeze.*)

JANE. I'll be with you in a second, Signor. I'm just having a little trouble with this mannequin.

(*SHE re-attaches Paul's stocking and snaps his garter. HE does a silent scream.*)

FRU FRU. Thees ees a truly amazing doll The coloring of-a the skeen. So real.

(FRU FRU is about to touch him when GEORGE, arguing noisily with SYBIL, appears from behind the screen, having been pushed out by SYBIL, who enters behind him HE is dressed in briefs, a glamorous after-shower wrap around his waist, and a mini happy coat. HE looks decidedly uncomfortable. N.B.—he has underdressed.)

FRU FRU. *(Seeing George.)* Ah!

(JANE steers FRU FRU to the chair, seats him and stands behind him.)

SYBIL. This is our "Treasure Hunt" line, Signor.

(SHE nudges George. SHE has coached him. HE does a pathetic parade.)

SYBIL. This is for the modest man. The beautifully embroidered top can be worn belted, or casually, as Giorgio is modelling here.
FRU FRU. *(In Italian.)* Don't let the jealous husband catch you in that outfit, Giorgio. *[Giorgio, è meglio ch'l cornuto non ti trovo vestito cosi.]*

(GEORGE laughs nervously and looks to Sybil for help.)

SYBIL. When he has warmed up a little—

(SHE nudges George. HE starts to shiver fervently.)

SYBIL   *(Pointedly, to George.)* The top can be removed.

(GEORGE grudgingly removes it.)

SYBIL. Here you can see the matching loin cloth as we start to reveal the real animal.

(GEORGE growls at Sybil. SHE smiles sweetly. HE parades a little more, growling throughout.)

SYBIL. The cut of the wrap gives us a hint of what's to come.

(SHE looks at George meaningfully. HE reluctantly does a quick flash on either side of the loincloth, a peak at the bum, and twirls. JANE has covered her head in her hands. PAUL, throughout, has been trying to contain himself, but audibly lets go a bit. FRU FRU turns to see where the noise has come from. PAUL freezes.)

SYBIL. *(Quickly.)* And finally, for the truly daring man, the pièce de résistance.
GEORGE. *(Sotto voce.)* No.
SYBIL. *(Frozen smile.)* The pièce de résistance.

(SHE looks and gestures to GEORGE, who shakes his head. SHE rips off the loincloth. HE is now in a very daring pair of string bikini briefs. GEORGE covers his

*crotch with his hands, covers his cheeks, his nipples,
doesn't know what to do.)*

FRU FRU. Giorgio ees-a very shy for a model, no? Een
fact, he does not look like a model He is-a very old, no?
(Pointing at George's middle) And I never see a model
before with-a, how you say, handlebars

*(PAUL titters. GEORGE shoots him a frosty glance and
sucks in his stomach.)*

SYBIL. *(Improvising)* Actually, we chose Giorgio
specifically because we're aiming at a wider market. So to
speak. *(GEORGE puts on his robe.)* We wanted to show
how our designs could appeal to all men.
    FRU FRU. 'ow clever you are. You know, I am-a so
tired of-a always seeing the same-a models—gorgeous
men with-a all these-a muscles 'ow do you call them?
Cheese-a-steak?
    SYBIL. Beef-a-cake. And notice how well Giorgio's
ensemble ties in with the one Paul—ette is wearing.
    FRU FRU. Who ees-a Paulette?
    JANE. Oh—uh, that's just our pet name for our
mannequin.
    FRU FRU. Paulette. A beautiful name. For a beautiful
doll.
    JANE. *(Admiring Paul.)* Yes, she certainly is lovely,
isn't she? *(PAUL glares at Jane.)* How about some more
champagne, Signor?
    FRU FRU. Good idea I would like-a to propose a toast.
(To George, in Italian.) Giorgio, would you do the honors?
[Giogio, fai gli onori di casa?]

(GEORGE stares at Fru Fru uncomprehendingly.)

FRU FRU. *(Italian.)* Would you pour everyone a glass of champagne? *[Giorgio, puoi versare un bicchiere di champagne per tutti?]*

(Still nothing.)

FRU FRU. *(Italian.)* Champagne, you moron, pour the champagne! *[Champagne, imbecile! Metti il champagne!]*

PAUL. *(Hissing to George.)* Champagne!

GEORGE. Oh, Champania! Si, si. *(Over the next few lines, GEORGE pours and serves the champagne.)*

FRU FRU. Ladies, your designs are-a magnifico! The most exciting thing I 've-a seen in-a years *(With a look to Paul.)* Almost. *(Turns back.)*

GEORGE. *(Hands FRU FRU his champagne. Italian.)* Imbecile.

FRU FRU. *Grazie.* *(To Jane and Sybil.)* I theenk-a you 'ave a great future ahead of you. I like-a the way you do business. You have so much energy—so much enthusiasm—so much, 'ow do you say? So much funk.

SYBIL. Spunk.

FRU FRU. Si. Spunk. To Passion Fashion Wear! *(Handing glasses to JANE and SYBIL.)* May our relationship be a long and-a prosperous one!

JANE and SYBIL. *(Clinking glasses with Fru Fru, stunned.)* To Passion Fashion Wear!

(THEY drink.)

SYBIL. You mean we have a deal?

FRU FRU. We 'ave a deal—

(JANE and SYBIL jump for joy, ad-libbing—"That's wonderful!" "Thank you so much!" "We did it!" "I can't believe it!" etc. THEY hug and kiss one another, then FRU FRU. GEORGE and PAUL celebrate briefly.)

FRU FRU On-a one condition. *(EVERYBODY stops in their tracks.)* You must-a let me take-a this doll back home with-a me.

PAUL. *(Horrified.)* Ah!

GEORGE. *(Attempting to cover it up.)* Choo!

FRU FRU. Bless-a you

JANE. Oh, Signor, I'm afraid that's impossible. We couldn't part with Paul. Ette. Take something else. Take anything—take Giorgio!

SYBIL. Jane!

FRU FRU. I'm-a sorry, ladies. No doll, no deal.

(There is a KNOCK at the door.)

SYBIL. Who could that be?

JANE. I have no idea. Whoever it is, get rid of him, will you, Giorgio?

GEORGE. Right. I mean, si. *(GEORGE crosses to answer the door.)*

SYBIL. *(To Fruferelli.)* I'm very sorry, Signor, but I couldn't ask Jane to part with Paulette. She's very attached to him. Her. It.

FRU FRU. I'm very sorry, Signora, but I must 'ave-a Paulette.

(GEORGE opens the door. It's HODGE. GEORGE screams and tries to shut the door. EVERYONE turns to see what the commotion is.)

HODGE *(Forcing his way in, HE grabs George)* A-HA!! Caught you with your pants down!

(During the following, PAUL takes the odd breather when the attention is focussed away from him, snapping back into position when necessary)

HODGE. Thought you could outsmart me, did you? Thought you'd get away with it, did you? You petty thieves are all alike. So predictable. Never satisfied with your first haul. Always returning to the scene of the crime. Well I've got you now, and this time, I'm not letting go. *(HODGE sees Paul.)* Hello, sweetheart.

(PAUL offers Hodge a surreptitious wave. FRU FRU turns around to see who Hodge is talking to. PAUL freezes.)

FRU FRU. What ees-a thees?
HODGE. *(To George.)* Where's your friend?

(GEORGE shakes his head.)

HODGE. It'll be easier for you if you tell me now.

(GEORGE looks to Paul, thinks better of it, shakes his head again.)

FRU FRU. What ees-a going on?

SYBIL. It's all a mistake, Signor. *(To Hodge.)* Mr. Hodge, we're very grateful for your diligence, but really, this is all quite unnecessary.

HODGE I'm afraid it's very necessary. This man broke into this room and stole your underwear.

SYBIL. Lingerie.

FRU FRU. What?

JANE. No, no, no, like my partner says, it was all a misunderstanding. We don't want to press charges Couldn't we just forget about the whole thing?

HODGE. I'm afraid it's too late for that. Besides theft, I've still got him on breaking and entering, public mischief, assault and resisting arrest.

SYBIL. Look, can't you just drop it? It's not as if anyone was hurt, or anything.

HODGE. A couple of hours ago, you wanted me to lock this man up. Now you're protecting him. Is he a burglar, or isn't he?

JANE. No.

HODGE. Then why was he taking your things out of the room?

SYBIL. *(Quickly.)* To air them out.

HODGE. Air them out?

JANE. Yes, you see, they'd been sitting in the trunk of the car, next to all this fishing equipment, and they were starting to smell a bit—fishy

HODGE. I'll say. *(To Sybil.)* Then why did you say he was a burglar?

SYBIL. We thought he was at the time

HODGE. But you don't think that now.

SYBIL Of course not

HODGE. (*Sarcastically*) Then I suppose he is your husband, after all.

FRU FRU. Husband??

SYBIL. NO! He's my brother.

FRU FRU Brother???

HODGE. But you said you'd never seen him before in your lives.

JANE. That's true! They were separated at birth. He's her long-lost brother Giorgio.

SYBIL. From Italy.

GEORGE. Si, Italia. Pavarotti. Rigatoni. Frank Sinatra.

(FRU FRU gives George a look.)

HODGE. So who was the other bloke?

JANE. His twin.

SYBIL. Guiseppe.

HODGE. (*Indicating Fru Fru.*) Oh. And I suppose this is Chef Boy-ar-dee?

FRU FRU. Who?

JANE. Mr. Hodge, I know it sounds a little implausible, but—

HODGE. Implausible? Not at all. It makes perfect sense to me. (*To Sybil.*) Your long-lost twin brothers, Giorgio and Guiseppe from Italy, break into your room without your knowledge to air out your fishy underwear—

SYBIL. Mr. Hodge—

HODGE. Look, I don't want to hear it I'm getting too old for this nonsense I've worked here for twenty-five years, and I haven't seen a day like this since those weight watchers raided the Death by Chocolate convention But this—this takes the cake *(To George.)* First I have you and your "twin brother" trying to make off with a bundle of women's underwear, then I am rendered unconscious, face-down on a dessert trolley, and when I come to, I find myself nose to nose with a six-foot rabbit.

SYBIL. You'd just been knocked out—maybe you were seeing things

HODGE That's what I thought—until we started getting complaints from the guests about a man running around the hotel in nothing more than a pair of bunny ears and a little fuzzy tail.

FRU FRU. Yes, I saw him-a too! He tried-a to steal-a my coat!

JANE. You're kidding.

FRU FRU. And I never-a saw such ugly shorts.

SYBIL. *(With a look of triumph to Jane.)* Quite.

FRU FRU. The man ees a menace.

HODGE. Well, don't you worry. I'll track him down as soon as I'm finished with this one. Come along, "Giorgio."

(There is a KNOCK on the door.)

JANE. Who on earth could that be?

(SYBIL crosses and opens the door. It's SEBASTIAN, dressed in Paul's fishing outfit. The clothes are much too small for him.)

SEBASTIAN Hi. I'm sorry to bother you, but—(*HE sees Hodge and lowers his head nervously*)

HODGE. (*Crossing to Sebastian, dragging GEORGE with him and giving him the once-over.*) Hallo, hallo, hallo. Haven't we met ?

SEBASTIAN. (*Keeping his face averted.*) No, I don't think so.

HODGE. I'm sure we have. I never forget a face. What's your name?

SYBIL. (*To the rescue.*) Oh, how rude of me. I should have introduced you. Mr. Hodge, this is— this is—

JANE. Frederique!

SEBASTIAN. What?

SYBIL. That's right, Frederique What. Son. Watson.

JANE. Giorgio's lover!

(*SEBASTIAN and GIORGIO stare at one another in horror. GEORGE very slowly and reluctantly puts his arm around Sebastian and blows him a kiss. SEBASTIAN shrinks away.*)

GEORGE. (*With a lisp.*) How was the fishing, Frederique?

SEBASTIAN. Fishing?

(*PAUL does an elaborate mime of casting and reeling in. SEBASTIAN sees this and stares at Paul EVERYONE turns to look, and PAUL freezes in an improbable position.*)

SEBASTIAN. (*Uncertainly.*) Oh, fishing.

GEORGE. (*Indicating Seb's outfit.*) Yes, you've obviously borrowed *someone's* gear to go fishing, remember?

SEBASTIAN. (*Still unsure*) Right.

GEORGE. And now you've come back to get *changed*, haven't you?

SEBASTIAN *(Gratefully.)* YES'!! *(HE steps DS toward Sybil and Jane.)* I'll just get my things *(HE turns U.S. To George)* They're in the bathroom.

(As SEBASTIAN turns U.S. EVERYONE sees that his pants have split up the back and his bunny tail is protruding THEY all gasp and point. SEBASTIAN turns to them.)

FRU FRU. Eet's-a the bunny'

HODGE. Hold it right there! *(HE marches over to Sebastian, dragging GEORGE with him.)*

HODGE. (*Grabbing Sebastian.*) I thought you looked familiar. *(HE handcuffs George and Sebastian together)* Well, I've just about caught my limit, haven't I? Come along, you two Let's take you downstairs and get you weighed.

SEBASTIAN. It's not how it looks! I was just doing my job!

HODGE. I beg your pardon?

SEBASTIAN. (*Showing his bunny tail to Hodge.*) They made me put this on, *(Indicating George.)* and then he tried to get me involved in a threesome—

SYBIL. What??

HODGE. Look, I don't want to hear the sordid details about your love life.

SEBASTIAN. It wasn't my fault, I'm telling you.

HODGE. I don't care whose fault it was. I should have guessed you were mixed up with this bunch. I'm taking you in for indecent exposure, and (*Indicating Fru Fru.*) attempting to rob this man of his coat. (*Takes to Sebastian's outfit.*) By the way, where did you steal the fishing gear?

SEBASTIAN. I didn't steal it! (*Points toward the balcony.*) I was out by the pool and it fell from the sky!

HODGE. Now I've heard everything. Come on. (*HODGE marches THEM toward the door.*)

SYBIL. (*Changing tack.*) Mr. Hodge, please. Surely we can come to some sort of arrangement—

HODGE. I hope you're not suggesting a bribe, Mrs. Brunt, because I can't be bought.

SYBIL. No, not at all, I just meant that we should be able to work this out—

FRU FRU. I'M A-sorry, but you'll have to work it out without-a me. I have to catch-a my plane. Do I take-a Paulette with me, or no?

JANE. Uh—

(*SHE looks to Paul HE looks back, pleading silently.*)

FRU FRU. (*Walking over to Paul.*) I 'ave to 'ave 'er.

JANE. (*Looks helplessly to Paul, shrugs.*) OK. She's yours.

PAUL. (*Falsetto.*) NOOOOOOOOO!!!!!!!!!!

FRU FRU. (*Jumping out of his skin.*) WAAAAHHHHH!!!!!

GEORGE. You see, Signor Fruferelli, you can't have her. She's a real person—(*Italian accent.*) I mean, a real-a person.

SYBIL. And she's married—to him. (*SHE points to Hodge.*)

FRU FRU. Holy sheet!

HODGE. This gets better by the minute! I'll be right back after I've locked these two up for safe keeping.

SEBASTIAN. No, please don't leave me alone with him, that's just what he wants.

SYBIL. What?

HODGE. I won't be a moment ladies. And when I return, someone had better be ready to tell me the truth. (*HE opens the main door.*)

GEORGE. FOR GOD'S SAKE, PAUL, do something! I mean—Paulette-a do-a some-a thing!

HODGE. (*To Paul.*) See you in a minute, "Mrs Hodge!"

(HODGE leads GEORGE and SEBASTIAN off.)

FRU FRU. Mama Mia.

FRU FRU. And-a now, eef-a you weel excuse-a me, I must go. (*Looks to Paul.*) Weethout-a the doll. (*HE stands.*)

JANE. You're leaving?

FRU FRU. I 'ave to.

SYBIL. But what about our deal? You must give us a chance to explain, Signor.

FRU FRU. I cannot miss my plane.

SYBIL. It'll only take a moment.

FRU FRU. (*Checks his watch.*) OK. Uno momento.

SYBIL. Uh—(*SHE looks to Jane for help.*)

JANE (*Improvising.*) You see, Signor Fruferelli, Paulette is a life model. She poses as a mannequin for a living. She's quite famous, actually. And very expensive (*Smiles at Paul.*) We felt you deserved the finest money could buy. We only wanted to impress you

FRU FRU. Then-a why did you not tell-a me?

JANE. Well, uh ...

SYBIL. (*Coming to her rescue.*) We couldn't!' Paulette wouldn't allow us. It's written in her contract. She takes great pride in her work. We didn't mean to deceive you— but we really had no choice. Do you understand?

JANE. She's the best there is, Signor Fruferelli. And we wanted only the best for you.

(*HE considers. JANE and SYBIL hold their breath.*)

FRU FRU. I understand (*To Paul.*) A contract is a contract. Of-a course I cannot take you with me—what would I say to my wife? Heh heh!

(*FRU FRU heads for the door. EVERYONE follows him.*)

SYBIL. Uh, Signor—about *our* contract ...

FRU FRU. (*Stops at the door, and turns to Jane and Sybil. Smiling oilily.*) Surely, ladies, my word ees-a good enough.

SYBIL. (*With a look to Jane.*) Of course it is, Signor, but this is a multi-million dollar deal. We must have something in writing, don't you think?

FRU FRU (*Sighing heavily*) Eef you eenseest (*HE pulls a contract out of his briefcase.*) And-a now, I really must go.

(*SYBIL takes the contract and glances at it. JANE crosses to her and looks over Sybil's shoulder.*)

JANE. Signor Fruferelli, you've already signed this!

FRU FRU. Si, bellissima.

SYBIL. If you've already signed the contract, why did you come all this way to meet with us?

FRU FRU. Eet ees-a my way. I knew I wanted your-a designs—but I needed to know if I could-a work with-a you Now I know that I can. You are both-a so honest.

(*JANE and SYBIL take to each other.*)

JANE. Honest?

FRU FRU. Si. You 'ave-a to be. You are the worst liars I 'ave ever met een-a my life. (*HE laughs.*)

SYBIL. We'll take that as a compliment.

JANE. So, we have a deal? For real?

FRU FRU. For real. We 'ave a deal.

SYBIL and JANE. (*Delighted, embracing each other and Fruferelli.*) Thank you, Signor Fruferelli! Thank you so much!

FRU FRU. Arrivederci ladies, and-a thank-a you for everything. I weell-a be in touch. (*HE turns to go. Stops.*) Oh, please-a say good-bye to Giorgio for me—and-a tell him to lose a few pounds, will you? He'll get more work! (*To Paul.*) And-a to you, *mia cara,* you are a true artist— the best I 'ave ever seen. Eef-a you come to Italy, I will-a make you a star. Ciao! (*Kisses Paul's hand. PAUL wipes it off behind his back.*)

SYBIL. (*Opening main door.*) We'll walk you down to the limo, Signor.

FRU FRU. You are-a too kind. (*HE takes a step, stops, turns to Paul.*) Oh—I must apologize for ... (*Miming his "Woo Woo" bit perilously close to Paul's breasts.*) "Woo Woo!"

PAUL (*Falsetto.*) Oh, that's alright.

(*As FRU FRU crosses to the door, PAUL grabs him by the buns.*)

PAUL. (*Falsetto.*) Woo Woo!

FRU FRU. (*Laughing as he exits.*) Ciao! Woo Woo! (*HE exits.*)

PAUL. (*Kicking off his shoes.*) Torture. Absolute torture. (*Bends over to massage his calves.*)

(*The main door opens and HODGE enters. HE admires the view.*)

HODGE. Left you all alone, did they, Mrs. Hodge?

PAUL. (*Whipping around.*) What? (*Falsetto.*) What?

HODGE. We are supposed to be married aren't we? That's what your friend Mrs. Brunt claims, anyway.

PAUL. (*Falsetto.*) Oh, that. She was just a little confused. She's been under a lot of stress lately.

HODGE. Evidently. I'd like to speak to her, actually. I'd like to get to the bottom of this mess.

PAUL. (*Falsetto, trying to get rid of him.*) Well, she may be gone for quite some time. Why don't you come back later?

HODGE. (*Sitting.*) That's alright, I don't mind waiting.

PAUL. (*Falsetto.*) What about those two criminals? Don't you have to fingerprint them, or something?

HODGE. Oh, they're alright I locked them in my office for the time being.

PAUL. (*Falsetto.*) Is that safe?

HODGE. Perfectly. (*Jangling a key ring on his belt.*) I'm the only one who has a key.

PAUL. (*Takes to the keys. Face front.*) Ah-hah! (*Thinks for a moment.*) Well, as you could be waiting a while, you might as well make yourself comfortable.

HODGE. Good idea. (*HE takes off his clip-on tie and stuffs it in his pocket.*) That's better.

PAUL. (*Falsetto.*) Wouldn't you feel better taking off your shoes? Your jacket? Your *belt*?

HODGE. No, no. I'm alright, thanks.

PAUL. (*Under his breath.*) This is going to be tougher than I thought.

HODGE. What was that?

PAUL. (*Falsetto.*) Uh—I said, "I'm so glad those ruffians were caught."

HODGE. That makes two of us. It's been quite a day.

PAUL. (*Falsetto.*) Yes, you've really had your hands full, haven't you? (*Pouring two glasses of champagne.*) I think you deserve a drink.

HODGE. Oh no, I can't drink on duty.

PAUL. (*Falsetto, flirting.*) You wouldn't let a lady drink alone, would you?

HODGE. (*Weakening.*) It's against regulations.

PAUL. (*Falsetto, fluttering his eyelashes.*) Just this once? I won't tell.

HODGE (*Flustered.*) You promise?

(*PAUL mimes zipping his lips.*)

HODGE. Alright, a small one.

PAUL. (*Falsetto*) Fine. (*HE hands HODGE a tumbler full of champagne.*) Bottoms up!

HODGE. Cheers.

(*PAUL sits very close to Hodge. THEY clink glasses and drink.*)

PAUL. (*Falsetto.*) I love a man with a big bunch of keys. It's so masculine. (*HE plays with the keys.*) You must be very important, having access to so many places.

HODGE. (*Flattered.*) Well, it is a big responsibility ...

PAUL. (*Falsetto, tugging at the keys.*) There are so many of them! How do you keep track of them all?

HODGE. (*Taking keys from Paul and giving him a playful tap on the wrist.*) What are you looking for? The key to my heart?

(PAUL giggles to Hodge, *turns away and the giggle turns into a groan.*)

PAUL. (*Falsetto.*) I can't help myself—I'm crazy for men in uniform.

HODGE. And how do you feel about men out of uniform?

PAUL. (*Falsetto, shocked*) Mr Hodge! What are you implying?

HODGE. I ᴄould ask you the same question.

PAUL. (*Falsetto.*) What do you mean?

HODGE. Well, you sit me down, fill me with champagne, play with my keys and start going on about my uniform. I mean, what's a man to think?

(PAUL opens his mouth to argue and stops. HE realizes what he has to do. HE takes a healthy swig from the bottle of champagne.)

PAUL. (*Falsetto.*) You're right. I can't deny it. I want you.

HODGE. (*Gulps.*) Really?

PAUL. (*Falsetto.*) Really.

HODGE. Right then. (*HODGE begins to undo his belt, not taking his eyes off Paul.*)

PAUL. (*Terrified.*) What are you doing?

HODGE. (*Takes off the belt, pulls out the radio.*) Just getting some business out of the way.

(HE tosses the belt—with the keys still attached—on the couch. PAUL's eyes are glued to it.)

HODGE. (*Into radio.*) Fred, Rodge Hodge here. I'm in 504 if you need me. Emergencies only. (*HE tosses the radio on the couch and advances on PAUL, who backs away.*) Don't be nervous, I won't bite.

PAUL. (*Falsetto.*) Good, good.

HODGE. (*Pursuing him around the room.*) Unless you want me to, that is.

(PAUL whimpers.)

HODGE. Well, what do you fancy? *(Indicating bedroom.)* The waterbed? *(Indicates the balcony.)* Al fresco?

PAUL. *(Discovers himself at the bathroom door, opens it. Falsetto.)* How about the shower? *(HE shoves HODGE into the bathroom, slams the door, opens it again. Falsetto.)* I'll be right there! *(HE closes the door, takes a step, stops and opens it again. Falsetto.)* Don't start without me!

(HE slams the door and dives for the keys. HE picks them up and reaches the main door as it is flung open. HE is caught behind it. JANE and SYBIL enter.)

JANE. ... and he wants us to come to *Milan* for his fashion show! I hope Paul can get the time off work.

SYBIL. I hope he can get George out of jail. Where is everybody?

(The door slowly closes and PAUL appears, keys in hand.)

PAUL. Shhhh!!
JANE. What are you doing now?
PAUL. SSHHH!! Hodge is in the bathroom.
SYBIL. What's going on?
PAUL. Never mind—there's no time to explain. We've got to get out of here. George and Sebastian are down in Hodge's office. *(HE holds up the keys.)* I've got the keys.

SYBIL. How did you manage that?
PAUL. Don't ask. Let's just go.
SYBIL. GIVE ME THE KEYS. (*PAUL hands them to her.*)

(*As THEY head for the door, the bathroom door opens. SYBIL exits smartly. JANE, unable to reach the door, jumps behind the screen. HODGE enters, a towel around his waist, still wearing his shoes and socks.*)

HODGE. What's taking you so long?

(*PAUL, trapped wheels around, SLAMS the door shut.*)

HODGE. It's getting pretty steamy in there.
PAUL. (*Falsetto.*) I can imagine.
HODGE. Who was that?
PAUL. (*Falsetto.*) What? Oh, just the maid. I sent her away.
HODGE. (*Fantasizing.*) That's a pity. You should have invited her in. I've never been to an orgy.

(*HODGE advances toward Paul. PAUL cringes.*)

HODGE. (*Indicates the bathroom.*) Shall we?
PAUL. (*Falsetto.*) No! Uh, Mr. Hodge—
HODGE. Please call me Rodge.
PAUL. (*Falsetto, through gritted teeth.*) Rodge—before we get too—umm—involved, I think I should tell you—I may not be what you're expecting ... I mean, I may be quite a—disappointment to you.
HODGE. There's nothing about you that could disappoint me.

PAUL. (*Falsetto, looks down.*) Believe me, there is.
HODGE. I'll take my chances.

(*HODGE advances toward Paul, backs him over the edge of the couch and is about to kiss him.*)

PAUL. (*Cringing, HE manages to squeak out.*) Help!
JANE. (*Appearing from behind the screen.*) Mr. Hodge!

(*PAUL and HODGE take to Jane in astonishment.*)

HODGE. (*Releasing Paul.*) Please, it's not what you think!
JANE. Oh really?
HODGE. I can explain ...
JANE. Don't bother. I was right here. I heard everything.
HODGE. Everything?
JANE. You should be ashamed of yourself, Mr. Hodge. I'm going to complain to the management.
HODGE. No, please, don't do that! I'm only six months from an early retirement!
JANE. (*Heading for the phone.*) You should have thought of that before.
HODGE. Please! I couldn't help myself—I was overcome with lust. (*PAUL groans*) Please, I'll do anything you say!
PAUL. Anything?
HODGE. Name it.
JANE. (*Crossing to him.*) Alright. I think we can come to an arrangement. If you'll agree to free those two

prisoners of yours, we promise we'll never speak of this to anyone.

HODGE. I can't do that—that's blackmail!

JANE. (*Crossing to the phone.*) Suit yourself.

HODGE. Alright! Alright! It's a deal.

(THEY shake.)

JANE. Wow. Two in one day!

(The door opens. SYBIL enters, followed by GEORGE and SEBASTIAN, un-handcuffed.)

SYBIL. (*Taking in the scene.*) Well, well, well! Never a dull moment.

HODGE. (*Seeing George and Sebastian.*) What are you two doing here?

GEORGE and SEBASTIAN. (*Bolting for the door.*) AAAGGHH!!

JANE. George, Sebastian, it's alright. Come back. Mr. Hodge has very kindly agreed to let you go. Haven't you, Mr. Hodge?

HODGE. Um—

SEBASTIAN. Good. I'll be getting dressed if anybody needs me. (*HE scuttles unnoticed into the bathroom.*)

JANE. Mr. Hodge? That is our deal, isn't it?

HODGE. (*Humbly.*) Yes.

SYBIL. Will someone please tell me what's going on?

JANE. Just a little collective bargaining.

GEORGE. (*To Hodge.*) It took me a moment to recognize you—out of uniform.

HODGE. (*Checks himself and realizes*) Uniform! Excuse me—(*HE dashes into the bathroom and closes the door.*)

SYBIL. What happened to Sebastian?

(*There is a SCREAM. The bathroom door opens and SEBASTIAN enters, clutching his clothes, dressed only in the bunny briefs.*)

SEBASTIAN. I've had some weird gigs before, but this beats them all.

JANE. Look, Sebastian, we're really sorry about all this. We'll make it up to you somehow.

SEBASTIAN. I don't think that's possible.

GEORGE. Let me write you a cheque—

SEBASTIAN. STAY away from me, you. I've had enough of your advances for one day.

(*SYBIL whacks George on the arm.*)

JANE. Sebastian, please, we insist.

SEBASTIAN. Forget the money. This one's on the house. (*HE crosses to the main door, stops.*) I'll mail you the bunny ears. (*HE exits.*)

SYBIL. Jane, how did you manage to convince Hodge to drop the charges?

JANE. Simple. I waited until he'd compromised himself with "poor Paulette" and then I made a deal with him. I'm getting to be pretty good at that.

SYBIL. (*To Paul.*) But why were you in that get-up to begin with?

PAUL. (*Indicating the bathroom.*) I was hiding from Don Juan!

SYBIL. In a Merry Widow and heels?

PAUL I'll explain later.

JANE. I can hardly wait.

GEORGE Do you mind if I get dressed first?

SYBIL (*Crossing behind screen to fetch his clothes.*) Good idea. We have some serious celebrating to do.

GEORGE. And we have some serious apologizing to do.

SYBIL. (*Crossing to George and handing him his clothes.*) Don't think we don't know it.

HODGE. (*Enters in full uniform and heads for the main door.*) I'll be on my way now.

JANE. Mr. Hodge.

HODGE. Yes, ma'am?

JANE. Don't worry—your secret is safe with us. Enjoy your retirement.

HODGE. (*Subdued.*) Thank you.

PAUL. (*Falsetto.*) Mr. Hodge, don't be too hard on yourself. It could happen to anyone.

HODGE. I don't know what to say. It's just that when I saw you I lost my head. I'd never seen anyone I'd wanted that much in my life.

PAUL. (*Falsetto.*) You've got to get out more.

HODGE. I'm sorry. I think I'll get back to work now.

PAUL. (*Falsetto.*) Of course.

(*HE follows HODGE to the door, spots a pair of sequined bikini briefs and picks them up. HODGE opens the door.*)

PAUL. (*Falsetto.*) Rodge. (*HODGE turns.*) Here. Take these. (*HE hands him the briefs.*) Save them for a special occasion.

HODGE. Thank you.

(*PAUL blows HODGE a kiss. HODGE catches it and exits. SYBIL and GEORGE watch this in astonishment. PAUL collapses with a groan.*)

PAUL. Is there a chiropractor in the house?

JANE. Nurse Jane to the rescue!

(*SHE crosses to massage him. SYBIL leads GEORGE toward the bedroom.*)

SYBIL. Come along, Tarzan, let's get you back into your civvies. (*SHE looks him up and down.*) On second thought, maybe I should keep you like this. You're kind of cute in that outfit—handlebars and all.

GEORGE. Do you really think so?

SYBIL. Of course. I can hardly keep my hands off you.

GEORGE. Really?

(*SYBIL growls and chases GEORGE into the bedroom. PAUL and JANE watch them go.*)

PAUL. (*Moaning with pleasure.*) Thank you.

JANE. I don't know why I'm doing this. I should be strangling you instead. You nearly ruined everything.

PAUL. I know, your Honor, I'm guilty as charged. But I've paid my debt to society. (*HE removes his clip earrings.*) Ow!! Why in Heaven's name didn't you and Sybil just tell us about this Fruferelli thing in the first place?

JANE. We were going to tell you after we had closed the deal. We were going to surprise you with a big celebration

PAUL. (*Standing up and putting his arms around her*) I think we need a little celebration right now.

JANE. Now, don't go starting things you can't finish.

PAUL. Not to worry, this is just a taste. We'll finish up later

(*THEY kiss. HODGE comes in through the door, talking as he enters.*)

HODGE. Sorry to barge in, but I forgot my radio—oo—(*As HE notices the two "women" kissing.*) OOHHH MY GOD!

(*JANE and PAUL look at Hodge and freeze. Beat.*)

HODGE. (*Picking up radio and keying mike.*) Hello, Fred? This is Hodge. I'm knocking off early tonight. (*HE pulls out the fancy briefs that Paul gave him earlier.*) Special occasion!!

(*HODGE tosses the radio and advances toward Paul and Jane. HE exits and emits a deep-throated grunt of pleasure, waving the briefs in glee. THEY retreat slowly as—*)

THE CURTAIN FALLS

THE END

COSTUME PLOT

SYBIL
White satin blouse
Additional shoulder pads
Short pink tweed skirt
Black pumps w/ gold buckle
Black purse w/chain strap
Black sunglasses
Gold button earrings
Gold, black, pearl coin necklace
Fake Rolex watch

JANE
Black palazzo pants w/white pin dot
Wide black belt
Red cross-over body suit
Black patent pumps
Black handbag
Rhinestone earrings
Matching necklace
Man's watch

SEBASTIAN
Navy overcoat
Dark blue-gray pleated pants
Belt w/silver findings
Turquoise silk shirt
Black penny boxers w/fur sporran
Gray briefs w/bunny face and tail
Double w/face and tail reversed

Double Paul jeans (too short)
Double Paul shirt (too small)

HODGE
Navy blazer w/gold buttons
Navy pants w/satin stripe
White shirt (velcroed)
Clip-on red tie
Belt
Black shoes
White towel w/hotel insignia
White T-shirt
Watch

FRUFERELLI
White silk shirt
White pants
Yellow stripe suspenders
Pink socks
White shoes w/mesh front
Pale yellow ascot
White open-front smock
Cream wool overcoat
Cream straw hat
Watch

GEORGE
Gray striped polo shirt
Beige chinos
Black rubber boots
Fishing vest
Fishing hat w/lures

Balaclava
Plaid boxers
Peach satin negligee
Matching peignoir
Silver mules
Black wig
Leopard print briefs (doubles)
Red satin shower wrap
Black satin short kimono w/embroidered back
Black leather slippers

PAUL
Blue jeans
Red plaid shirt
Brown leather belt
Red baseball hat
Black socks
Rubber deck shoes
Big sombrero
White satin Merry Widow w/garter
Peach satin tap pants
Hot pink satin robe
White fish net stockings
Satin champagne pumps
Pearl drop earrings (clip-on)
Long red wig
Dance belt

PROPERTY PLOT

Love seat
Large chair
Coffee table
End table
Circular table
Tablecloth
Small chair
Clothing racks (on wheels)
Wardrobe screen (w/shelf, mirror and hook on back)
Mirror
Small/Tall table
Box full of hangers
Area rug
Door numbers (Room 504)
Phone (practical, hotel-style)
Phone (hidden on set to make the sound of the cellular phone)
Lots of lingerie (men's and women's)
8 x 10 photos (Sebastian, Peter, Cliff, and Forrest plus 15 others)
1 Cardboard box (#3) (thin lingerie style)
Hotel room key
American Express Card
Blood donor card
Fishing tackle box
Plastic baggie (in tackle box)
Video camera
VHS tape
2 Large artificial potted plants (for balcony, topiary style, light weight)

Cardboard box (#5) (thin lingerie style)

Cardboard box (#4) (thin lingerie style)

Datebook (medium size, black, smart)

Pen or pencil (w/pocket clip)

Briefcase or satchel (for Sebastian to be carrying)

Pin container/pin cushion (glued shut w/a few pins glued
    on top)

Rolls of money (outer bills should be real, the rest can be
    paper)

Female mannequins (should look like Jane & Sybil; the
    Sybil on should have a removable right hand)

Hair dryer (pistol style)

Toilet plunger

Cardboard box (1x1x1) for wigs

Fruit basket (not breakable)

Fake fruit (for basket)

Real fruit (2 apples)

Champagne bucket

2 Bottles of Dom Perignon (filled nightly w/ginger ale,
    bottles not corked)

10 Wigs (two on top for George & Paul, the rest are misc.)

4 Champagne glasses

3 Tumblers

Line of sheets (tied together, strong enough to be climbed
    down or swung on [w/rope inside])

Section of curtain material

Lipstick (red)

Binder of fabric sketches & swatches (not too large)

Cellular phone (flip open kind, not real)

Handcuffs (good type)

Contract

Key ring w/a great many keys (on dog clip so Hodge can
  attach to his pants)
Walkie-talkie (small enough to fit in pocket–makes
  sounds)
Empty lingerie box
Lingerie box #1
Lingerie box #6
Boxer shorts
Jumping jocks boxer shorts
Bottom half of long lingerie box

ONSTAGE PRESET

Box #6 (on floor beside phone table—full of female
  lingerie)
Datebook w/pen inside (on table)
Picture of Forrest (on top of datebook)
2 Pairs of boxer shorts (on top of picture of Forrest)
Jumping jocks (on table—across top)
Pictures of Peter, Cliff & Sebastian (beside datebook)
Telephone (beside pictures)
Sybil's purse w/money inside (hanging on back of small
  chair)
Small clothing rack (in front of screen)
Box of hangers (in front of screen)
Pin cushion (in box of hangers)
Paul's pink robe (behind screen)
Satin high heels (behind screen)
Red wig (behind screen)
Black bathroom slippers (behind screen)
False breasts (behind screen)
Cellular phone ringer (behind screen—make sure on hook)

Jane's purse w/money in it (on couch)
Anorexic undies (in couch)
8 x 10 photos (on coffee table)
Empty lingerie box (on step—SL)
Lingerie box full of female lingerie (on top of empty box)
8 x 10 photos (on side table against wall)
Jane's notebook and pen (beside 8 x 10 photos)
Large clothing rack on wheels
8 x 10 photos (on side table beside armchair)

WHO'S UNDER WHERE   ACT I PRESET

BEDROOM

BATHROOM

Clothing rack

Window

Small table with drawers
Mirror (on wall above)

2 Small trees
(potted)

BALCONY

End Table
Large Chair

Coffee table

Love Seat

Window

Wardrobe
Screen

Clothing rack

Small Chair
Round Table

MAIN DOOR

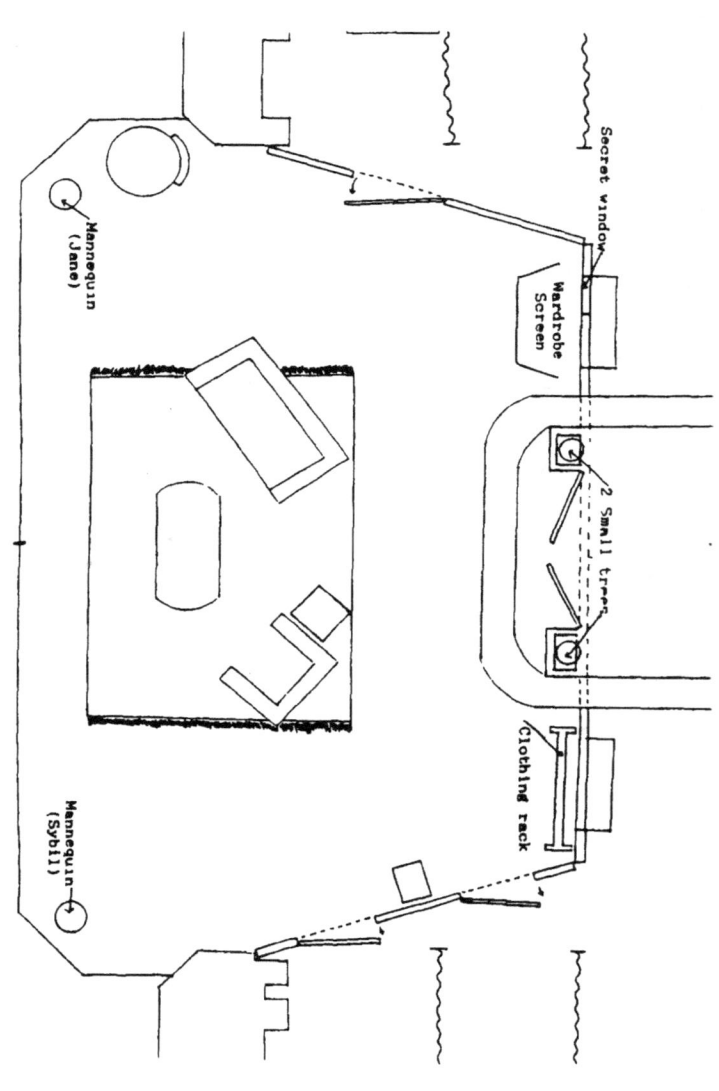

WHO'S UNDER WHERE - ACT II PRESET

Secret window

Wardrobe Screen

Mannequin (Jane)

2 Small trees

Clothing rack

Mannequin (Sybil)

OTHER TITLES AVAILABLE FROM SAMUEL FRENCH

CAPTIVE
Jan Buttram

Comedy / 2m, 1f / Interior

A hilarious take on a father/daughter relationship, this off beat comedy combines foreign intrigue with down home philosophy. Sally Pound flees a bad marriage in New York and arrives at her parent's home in Texas hoping to borrow money from her brother to pay a debt to gangsters incurred by her husband. Her elderly parents are supposed to be vacationing in Israel, but she is greeted with a shotgun aimed by her irascible father who has been left home because of a minor car accident and is not at all happy to see her. When a news report indicates that Sally's mother may have been taken captive in the Middle East, Sally's hard-nosed brother insists that she keep father home until they receive definite word, and only then will he loan Sally the money. Sally fails to keep father in the dark, and he plans a rescue while she finds she is increasingly unable to skirt the painful truths of her life. The ornery father and his loveable but slightly-dysfunctional daughter come to a meeting of hearts and minds and solve both their problems.

OTHER TITLES AVAILABLE FROM SAMUEL FRENCH

THE DECORATOR
Donald Churchill

Comedy / 1m, 2f / Interior

Marcia returns to her flat to find it has not been painted as she arranged. A part time painter who is filling in for an ill colleague is just beginning the work when the wife of the man with whom Marcia is having an affair arrives to tell all to Marcia's husband. Marcia hires the painter a part time actor to impersonate her husband at the confrontation. Hilarity is piled upon hilarity as the painter, who takes his acting very seriously, portrays the absent husband. The wronged wife decides that the best revenge is to sleep with Marcia's husband, an ecstatic experience for them both. When Marcia learns that the painter/actor has slept with her rival, she demands the opportunity to show him what really good sex is.

"Irresistible."
– *London Daily Telegraph*

"This play will leave you rolling in the aisles....
I all but fell from my seat laughing."
– *London Star*

OTHER TITLES AVAILABLE FROM SAMUEL FRENCH

THREE YEARS FROM "THIRTY"
Mike O'Malley

Comic Drama / 4m, 3f / Unit set

This funny, poignant story of a group of 27-year-olds who have known each other since college sold out during its limited run at New York City's Sanford Meisner Theater. Jessica Titus, a frustrated actress living in Boston, has become distraught over local job opportunities and she is feeling trapped in her long standing relationship with her boyfriend Tom. She suddenly decides to pursue her dreams in New York City. Unbeknownst to her, Tom plans to propose on the evening she has chosen to leave him. The ensuing conflict ripples through their lives and the lives of their roommates and friends, leaving all of them to reconsider their careers, the paths of their souls and the questions, demands and definition of commitment.